D0336784

# REPLICA

## GEMMA

# AUTHOR'S NOTE

Although in many cases you will find identical portions of dialogue occurring from both Gemma's and Lyra's perspectives in their respective narratives, you may also notice minor variations in tone and tempo. This was done deliberately to reflect their individual perspectives. Gemma and Lyra have unique conceptual frameworks that actively interact with and thus define their experiences, just as the act of observing a thing immediately alters the behavior of the thing itself.

The minor variations in the novel reflect the belief that there is no single objective experience of the world. No one sees or hears the same thing in exactly the same way, as anyone who has ever been in an argument with a loved one can attest. In that way we truly are inventors of our own experience. The truth, it turns out, looks a lot like making fiction.

Visit www.laurenoliverbooks.com for the latest news, competitions and exclusive material from Lauren Oliver.

# LAUREN OLIVER

# REPLICA

## GEMMA

HODDER &
STOUGHTON

# ONE

ESCAPE: THAT WAS WHAT GEMMA dreamed of, especially on nights like this one, when the moon was so big and bright it looked like it was a set piece in a movie, hooked outside her window on a curtain of dark night sky.

In movies, teenagers were always sneaking out. They'd wait until their parents went to bed, ease out from under their blankets already dressed in miniskirts and tank tops, slide down the stairs and unlatch the lock and *pop!* They'd burst out into the night, like balloons squeezing through a narrow space only to explode.

Other teenagers, Gemma guessed, didn't have Rufus: a seventy-five-pound retriever who seemed to consist entirely of fur, tongue, and vocal cords.

'Shhh,' Gemma hissed, as Rufus greeted her at the bottom of the stairs, wiggling so hard she was surprised he didn't fall over.

'Are you all right?'

She'd been awake for only a minute. But already her mother was at the top of the stairs, squinting because she didn't have her contacts in, dressed in an old Harvard T-shirt and sweatpants.

'I'm fine, Mom.' Gemma grabbed a glass from the cabinet. She would *never* sneak out. Not that she had anywhere to sneak out to, or anyone to sneak out with, since April's parents kept her just as leashed up as Gemma's did.

Still, she imagined for a second that she was halfway to the door, dressed in tight jeans and a shirt that showed off her boobs, the only part of her body she actually *liked*, on her way to hop in her boyfriend's car, instead of standing in a darkened kitchen in her pajamas at eleven p.m. on a Wednesday night while Rufus treated her ankles to one of his signature lick-jobs. 'Just needed some water.'

'Are you dehydrated?' Her mom said *dehydrated* as if it meant *dying*.

'I'm fine.' Gemma rattled the ice in her glass as she returned up the stairs, deliberately avoiding her mom's eyes. 'Go back to bed, okay?'

Her mom, Kristina, hesitated. 'Let me know if you need anything, okay?'

'Uh-huh.' Gemma shut her bedroom door in Rufus's face, not caring that he immediately began to whine. She set the water on her bedside table and flopped back onto the bed. The moon made squares on her bare legs, cutting her skin into portions of light and dark. She briefly let herself imagine what Chloe DeWitt and Aubrey Connelly were doing at that very second. She'd always been told she had a vivid imagination, but she just couldn't picture it. What was it like to be so totally, fundamentally, ruthlessly normal? What did they think about? What were their problems? Did they *have* any problems?

Rufus was still whining. Gemma got out of bed and let him in, sighing as he bounded immediately onto the bed and settled down exactly in the center of her pillow. She wasn't tired yet, anyway. She sat down instead at the vanity that had once belonged to her mother, an ornate Victorian antique she'd loved as a child and hadn't been able to tell Kristina she'd outgrown. She'd never been able to tell her parents much of anything.

The moon made hollows of her eyes in the mirror, turned her skin practically translucent. She wondered if this was how her parents always saw her: a half ghost, hovering somewhere between this life and the next.

But she wasn't sick anymore. She hadn't been sick in years, not since she was a little kid. Still, they treated her as if she might suddenly blow away, like a human house of cards, disturbed by the lightest touch.

She herself could barely remember all those years of sickness – the hospital, the operations, the treatments.

Coping, her therapist said. An *adaptive defense.*

She did remember a garden – and a statue, too. A kneeling god, she thought, but she couldn't be sure, with one arm raised to the sky, and the other reaching toward the ground, as though to draw something magic from the earth.

# TWO

GEMMA MUST HAVE BEEN THE only overweight sixteen-year-old girl in the entire history of the United States who actually *wished* she could participate in gym. It would be one thing if she were excused to go to study hall or free period. But due to 'scheduling limitations' (the stated reason) – or, as Gemma suspected, the innate sadism of Ms. Vicke, the vice principal – instead Gemma was forced to go to gym and sit in the bleachers, pretending to work, while the rest of her classmates zigzagged across the gym, their sneakers squeaking, or flew across the mulchy, wet soccer fields, running drills.

In the bleachers, there was nowhere to hide. She might as well be a blinking *Does Not Belong* sign. Even worse: Mrs. Coralee, the gym teacher (also a sadist – the school was full of them), insisted that Gemma change into the puckered nylon shorts and matching tank tops the whole class was forced to wear, which on Gemma only served to further underscore how little she belonged – like wearing full-on ski gear to the beach.

'You are so lucky.' April Ruiz, Gemma's best friend, swiped a lock of dark hair out of her eyes, as the girls filed back into the locker room. 'I'm pretty sure dodgeball was invented by the same people who thought up rectal thermometers and wool tights.'

'Move it, Frankenstein.' Chloe DeWitt jabbed an elbow, hard, in the space where Gemma's waist should have been, if she *had* a waist instead of a roll of flab. Gemma probably had forty pounds on Chloe, but the girl was all sharp corners and she knew how to use them to her advantage. Her elbows felt like whittled blades. 'Not *all* of us get to spend the whole period snacking.'

Gemma blushed. She had never, ever eaten in class. She had hardly ever eaten in the cafeteria, precisely so that Chloe, and girls like her, would never get the opportunity to make fun of her for it. But it didn't matter. From the time Gemma was little, Chloe had made it her mission to ensure that Gemma never forgot that she was a freak. In third grade, she'd hit on the name Frankenstein, after Gemma's second heart surgery had left her with a thick scar from her chest to her navel. After that, Gemma had never changed except in a bathroom stall – but no one at school besides April and her teachers ever called her anything else.

What Gemma couldn't understand was why – if she were so delicate, like her parents were saying (*you're delicate, Gemma, that's why we have to be so careful; no roller coasters, Gemma, your heart is delicate*) – she couldn't *look* delicate, like one of the small crystal animal figurines that her mom collected and kept enclosed in the corner cabinet, with legs as thin as toothpicks. Like Chloe, with a tan that appeared permanently shellacked to the contours of her body, as finely chiseled and well-tuned as an instrument. Like she had been formed by a god with an eye for detail, whereas Gemma had been slapped together haphazardly by a drunk.

'Yeah,' she muttered, as Chloe and her friends converged on the sinks, laughing. 'Lucky.'

'Don't let Cruella get to you,' April said in a low voice. April always took Gemma's side. Years ago, they had decided that either they were two aliens in a school of humans or possibly *the only two humans in a school of aliens.* 'Someone forgot to shoot her with her morning dose of tranquilizer.'

April and Gemma waited until Chloe and the pack of wolves – a fitting nickname for more than metaphoric reasons, since Gemma was fairly sure that Aubrey Connelly had had her incisors filed into points, and wouldn't have been surprised at all to learn that she liked the taste of human flesh – had changed before they stripped. They would both be late for study hall and would have to endure another lecture from Mr. Rotem. But anything was better than changing with the pack of wolves.

'Good news,' April said, when the rest of the locker room had cleared out. 'Mom finally caved on the Green Giant. I told her it wasn't *safe* to drive sixty miles in that beast, much less six *hundred*. How's that for strategy? I used her own psychology against her.'

'And so the hunted becomes the hunter,' Gemma said, in her best movie-announcer voice. Sometimes she thought her favorite part of the week was sitting on the wooden bench just outside the shower stalls, which hadn't been used in twenty years, talking with April while she washed her face and reapplied her makeup painstakingly, even though the result always made it look like she wasn't wearing any. Like they were in their own protected world. But not a world her parents had made for her. A world she'd *chosen*.

'Something like that. Anyway, we'll be cruising down to Florida in our very own Lexus. Can you believe it? My brother's *so* pissed.'

Apart from Gemma's, April's parents were the most protective people Gemma knew. Neither Gemma nor April was allowed to date – not that it mattered, since nobody wanted to date them. The list of other things they weren't allowed to do included, but was not limited to:

(1) stay up past ten o'clock; (2) attend any school events or dances unless they were in a large group of females only, which precluded them from going, since they had no other friends; (3) go to Raleigh unless April's brother, a senior, chaperoned; (4) be on Instagram.

Gemma was sure that even if she were five-eleven and a supermodel look-alike, her parents' absurd beliefs about social media (*It rots the brain! It's bad for self-esteem!*) would have ensured she stayed on the bottom of the social food chain. She was also sure that when her mom and April's got together, all they did was brainstorm elaborate and ever more absurd ways to make sure that both April and Gemma stayed safe, friendless except for each other, and totally miserable.

When half the junior girls decided to spend spring break in Miami, Gemma hadn't even bothered petitioning her parents to be allowed to go. She knew she had just about as much chance of being named the first female president of the United States . . . at age sixteen. Besides, she had no desire to spend her vacation bumping into the same predators she spent all her time deliberately avoiding at school.

But April – who was not only prettier, smarter, and far more optimistic than Gemma, so much so that had they not been absolute, sworn lifelong best friends, co-aliens, outcasts together, Gemma would have despised her – hadn't given in so easily. She'd begged her parents. She'd cried. She had thrown a tantrum – a risky proposition, since her mother, Angela Ruiz, a renowned prosecutor for the state, had been known to frighten grown men into confessions at their first meeting. (And her *other* mother, Diana, was a computer programmer who had won several kickboxing competitions in her early twenties.)

Then the miraculous had happened. April hit on the magic word: *sexism.*

It was *sexism*, April claimed, that her older brother, Ryan, got to go on spring break with his friends. It was *sexism* that he got to drive a Lexus while she was stuck with the Green Giant, an ancient chartreuse station wagon. And even though Ryan was two years older, and the Lexus had been a congratulations gift for getting into Harvard early action, suddenly April's moms had generated a counteroffer: April and Gemma could take the car and drive down to Bowling Springs, Florida, for a week, where April's grandparents lived.

Even better, they had convinced Gemma's parents that it was a good idea.

And, yeah, sure, maybe hanging out in a community known for its 65+ dating scene and competitive weekly badminton tournament wasn't exactly the spring break of every girl's dream. But it was better than nothing. They could stay for a whole nine days, paddle around the pool, walk down to the community tennis courts, and take their car to the beach. They could drink virgin piña coladas and sample fried gator at the local restaurants. Still better, they would have the house to themselves for three full days while April's grandparents were off attending some weird Positive Visualization Health Retreat that involved a lot of yoga and deep breathing – a minor detail Gemma had managed to avoid in all of her conversations with her parents.

Discussing spring break plans with her best friend made Gemma feel all-American, beauty-magazine, country-song normal. So much so that she wasn't sure she actually wanted to *go*, just so she could keep talking about it.

April had to hop, haul, and wiggle to get into her jeans. Her preferred fit, she always said, was *human sushi roll*. Gemma's was *airy trash bag*. 'I'll pick you up Saturday at eight a.m., got it?'

'Got it,' Gemma said. They'd agreed on Saturday, March 19, eight a.m. weeks ago, but reconfirmed almost every day. Why not? This was the first adventurous thing either of them had ever done in their lives, unless you counted microwaving Peeps at Easter to watch them explode.

Gemma wished she only felt excited. She wished, more than anything, that her parents' words and warnings hadn't over time worked their way like a virus into her cells, replicating there.

She wished she wasn't also just the littlest, tiniest bit scared.

But she told herself nothing would happen. After all, nothing ever did.

# THREE

A LIST OF ALL THE medical conditions Gemma had had since she was born:

1. two broken tibias
2. one collapsed lung
3. congenital heart failure
4. pneumonia
5. poison ivy (on her butt, of all places)
6. pneumonia again
7. a fractured wrist
8. hypothyroidism
9. pneumonia, a third time

A list of some of the medical conditions she had not had:

1. the bubonic plague
2. that disease where you stay really skinny, no matter how much you eat

Every so often, when Gemma approached the massive iron gates that encircled her property, she got a flash of something – not memory, exactly, but something close to it, like the sudden recollection of a song you heard someone sing only once. There was a high fence lost somewhere in the wild tangle of fever-dreams that had so often been hers as a very young child – a high fence, a giant statue of a man kneeling in the dirt, reaching, it seemed, simultaneously for heaven and hell.

The driveway was exactly one-quarter of a mile long. Gemma knew because one time she had asked her mom to measure it in the car. It bisected an enormous lawn spotted with ancient spruce trees and flowering dogwood. On days when April had chorus, taking the bus and walking the quarter mile up the driveway was infinitely preferable to having her dad's driver pick her up, which would require that she wait at the student drop-off area, in full view of the senior playing fields, and would be a tacit admission that she had only one friend to drive her.

Besides, it was practically the only exercise Gemma got. On nice days she walked deliberately slowly, making it last, enjoying the smell of freesia and honeysuckle and listening to the faint whine of the mosquitoes clustered in the shade.

Today, she walked quickly, too preoccupied by the plans for Saturday (*the day after tomorrow!*) – a ten-hour road trip, a real adventure, with her best friend – to care about the prettiness of the day. Because of the landscaping and the angle of the drive, she was practically on the front porch before she noticed two cop cars, one of which had its doors swinging open, as if the officers had been in too much of a hurry to bother closing them. Her mother was speaking to one of them, holding her throat with one hand.

*Dad,* Gemma thought immediately, and, without realizing it, broke into a run, her backpack jogging against her back.

'Gemma!' Kristina turned to stare as Gemma arrived in front of her, already panting, sweat gathering beneath the waistband of her jeans and trickling down her spine. She reached out and seized Gemma's shoulders. 'What's the matter? Is everything okay?'

Gemma stared. 'What do you mean, *is everything okay*?' She gestured to the cop cars, and the cop who stood a little ways apart from mother and daughter, hands on his hips, sunglasses on, staring up at the sky as though debating whether he might still get a tan at this angle. 'What's going on?'

'Oh.' Kristina exhaled long and loud, releasing Gemma's shoulder. 'This? It's nothing. Something stupid. A prank.'

By then, Gemma had noticed that one of the large glass panes of the French doors was shattered, as if something heavy had been hurled through it. She could see a second cop moving through the living room, placing his weight delicately, his footsteps making a *crunch-crunch* sound on the glass. As she watched, a third cop emerged, a woman, holding what at first appeared to be a lumpy rock in an improbable shade of green between two gloved hands. But as she shifted it to show her colleague, Gemma's whole body went cold. It wasn't a rock, but a Halloween Frankenstein mask stapled at the neck. From the way the cop was handling it, Gemma knew it must be heavy. It had obviously been filled with something to help it maintain its shape.

'Oh my God.' Gemma could feel the blood pounding in her temples. Chloe. That fucking bitch. She focused on thinking logically so that she wouldn't start to cry. How had it happened? How had Chloe arrived so much quicker than the bus? Could she have cut last period? No. Gemma had seen her getting into Aubrey's car. And how had they gotten past the gates? The whole property was fenced in. But she was sure Chloe and Aubrey were to blame, would have staked her life on it.

*Frankenstein.* The misshapen monster.

'It's all right, Gem. It's all *right*,' Kristina said, in a shrill voice, as if she didn't quite believe it. 'No one was hurt.'

That only made Gemma feel worse. *No one was hurt* meant *someone* could *have been hurt.* What if her mom had been in the living room? Unlikely, of course. Even though the house – Château Ives, as April called it, only half-jokingly – could have fit an army during wartime, her mom never went anywhere except her bedroom, the kitchen, the downstairs yoga studio, and the bathroom, as if she were controlled by a centrifugal force that kept her rotating between those four places. But what if Ender and Bean, their cats, had been curled up on the sofa? What if Rufus had been sunning himself on the rug?

'If you want us to file a report, we'll need you down at the station,' said the cop with sunglasses, the one who looked bored. But he was doing his best to be polite. The Ives family, he'd obviously been told, was important.

Kristina shook her head. 'I don't know,' she said. 'If only Geoff . . .' She trailed off. 'My husband is in a meeting,' she said, by way of explanation. Gemma's dad was always in a meeting, or in a car, or on a plane.

'How'd they get in?' Gemma blurted. The front gates could only be opened by a code. Guests had to be buzzed in. Château Ives meets Fort Knox.

Kristina blushed. Even when she blushed, she looked pretty. Gemma had tried for years to find herself in her mother's model-pretty face, in her high cheekbones and slender wrists. The most she could detect was a similar way of frowning. 'There were vendors in and out for Sunday's horse show,' she explained, half to Gemma, half to the police. 'Florists, the planner . . . I left the gates open so they wouldn't have to keep buzzing.'

Which no doubt meant: *I popped a Klonopin, had a glass of wine, and took a nap.* Since her parents never said exactly what they meant, Gemma had become adept at translating for them.

'Finke, look at this.' Yet another cop came jogging out of the front door. He, too, was wearing nylon gloves, and holding a note written on a scrap of paper between his pointer and middle fingers. 'This came with the special delivery.'

The bored-looking cop flipped his sunglasses to the top of his head and read without reaching for it. The message was short, but Gemma felt the anger roil inside of her, pulling her heart down to her toes.

*your sick your a monster you deserve to die*

Kristina gasped as though she'd been physically slapped. Finke nodded, and the other cop withdrew, bagging the note carefully in plastic. Gemma imagined seeing Chloe arrested, her hands wrenched behind her back, her face squashed against the top of a cop car. She imagined her thrown into jail for the rest of her life, bunking with a murderous boulder with a name like Princess.

She imagined wrapping her hands around Chloe's neck and watching it snap.

'I – I think I'd better come with you,' Kristina said. Now the blush was gone. She just looked pale, and confused. 'Who would *do* something like this? Who would be so *awful*?'

'Have you or your husband been having any problems lately?' Finke asked. 'Disputes? Legal issues?' Kristina shook her head.

'No other threatening messages, or phone calls?'

She again shook her head. 'I just can't *imagine* –'

'Mom, wait.' Gemma felt the words like nausea. *It's my fault. It's because everyone thinks I'm a freak.* Her mom knew that Gemma had a rough time in school, but Kristina's sympathy always made Gemma feel worse. The only thing more painful than being unpopular was being the unpopular daughter of a former popular girl. She took a deep breath. 'I know.'

'What?'

'I know who did it.' Now all the cops were watching her – pityingly, she thought. She felt her cheeks heating up and was absolutely positive she did not look pretty like her mom. When Gemma blushed, she looked as if two pigments were trying to throttle each other beneath her skin. 'It's just some stupid girl at school. She probably thought it'd be funny.'

Was it her imagination, or did her mom, just for the tiniest second, look relieved? 'Oh, honey,' she said, and started to put her arms around Gemma. Gemma side-stepped her.

'It's fine,' she said. 'I'm *fine*.'

'You still want to file the report?' Finke asked, but Gemma could tell he no longer thought it was a good idea. The whole vibe had changed. No one was looking at her. The cops were loading up, restless, eager to get back to more important things than some high school girl's social humiliation. Maybe they were annoyed they'd been dragged out here in the first place.

'It's up to you, sweet pea.' Kristina reached out and threaded her hand through Gemma's hair. 'What do you think?'

Gemma shook her head. As tempting as it was to imagine Chloe in a prison-orange jumpsuit — surely, surely, even Chloe wouldn't look good in prison orange — she knew that if she made a big deal out of it, things would only get worse. Then she'd be Frankenstein-the-Crybaby. The Alien Snitch.

Still, she felt the sudden, overwhelming desire to scream. Chloe and her little pack of wolverines had been doing their best to make Gemma miserable for years. But they had never done anything this bad. They'd come to her house. They'd taken the time to fill a Halloween mask with rocks or concrete rubble or metal shrapnel from their mechanical hearts. They had said that she deserved to die. Why? What had she ever done to them?

She was an alien, adrift on an unfriendly planet. Hopeless and lost.

'Are you sure?' Kristina said, smoothing Gemma's face with a thumb. Gemma was scowling.

She took a step backward. 'Positive,' she said.

'Okay.' Kristina exhaled a big breath and gave Finke a weak smile. 'Sorry for all the trouble. You know how girls are.'

'Mm-hmm,' he said, in a tone that he made it clear he didn't and had no desire to, either.

Gemma felt like going straight to her room, possibly forever, but Kristina managed to get an arm around her shoulders. For a thin woman, she was surprisingly strong, and she held Gemma there in a death grip.

'I'm sorry, honey,' she said. 'Why didn't you tell me you were having problems at school?'

She shrugged. 'It's no big deal.'

Kristina smelled, as always, like rose water and very

expensive perfume. So expensive that it actually smelled like new-printed money. 'I don't want your father to worry, do you?' She smiled, but Gemma read anxiety in her mother's eyes, decoded the words her mother would never say: *I don't want him to think you're more of a disappointment than he already does.* 'Let's just tell him there was an accident. A kid and a baseball. Something like that.'

To hit a baseball from the street through the living room window, the kid would have to be a first-draft pick for the major leagues. Usually her parents' willingness to lie about things big and small bothered Gemma. If her parents were so good at making up stories, how could she ever be sure they were telling the truth?

Today, however, she could only be grateful.

'Baseball,' she said. 'Sure.'

Gemma woke up in the middle of the night from a nightmare that, thankfully, released her almost as soon as she opened her eyes, leaving only the vague impression of rough hands and the taste of metal. In the hall, Rufus was whimpering.

'What's the matter?' she said, easing out of bed to open the door for him. As soon as she did, she heard it: the sudden swell of overlapping voices, the angry punctuation of silence. Her parents were fighting.

'It's okay, boy,' she whispered to Rufus, threading a

hand through the scruff of fur on his neck. He was a baby about fights. Immediately, he darted past her and leapt onto the bed, burying his head in her heap of pillows, as if to block out the sound from downstairs.

She would have gone back to bed, but at exactly that moment, her father's voice crested, and she very clearly heard him say, '*Frankenstein*. For Christ's sake. Why didn't you tell me?'

Gemma eased out into the hall, grateful for the plush rug that absorbed the sound of her footsteps. Quickly, she moved past paneled squares of moonlight, past guest rooms always empty of guests and marble-tiled bathrooms no one ever used, until she reached the main staircase. Downstairs, a rectangle of light yawned across the hallway. Her father's study door was open, and Gemma got a shock. Her mother was perched on the leather ottoman, her face pale and exhausted-looking, her arms crossed at the waist to keep her bathrobe closed. Gemma had never, ever seen anyone besides her father in the study. She had always assumed no one else was allowed to enter.

'I tried calling. . . .' Her mother's voice was weak and a little bit slurred, as if all the edges were lopped off. It must be after midnight. He must have woken her up from a sleeping-pill slumber.

'Feeding me some bullshit story. I had to hear it from Frank at the department. Thank God *someone* respects me.'

Gemma's heart sank. It had been stupid to believe that they could conceal the truth from her father. He had contacts everywhere – in the police department and even in the government, although he kept his most important contacts secret. He'd cofounded the sixth-largest pharmaceutical company in the country, Fine & Ives, which made everything from shampoo to heart medication to drugs for soldiers suffering from PTSD. Although he'd been kicked off the board of his own company after a brutal three-year legal battle when Gemma was a toddler – Gemma had never found out the details, but she knew her dad had disapproved of where the company was putting its resources – he still traveled with a personal security guard and went to Washington, DC, every quarter to meet with politicians and lobbyists and top brass.

Often Gemma feared she would never, ever get truly away from her parents – not even when she went to college, not even when she moved out and moved as far away from Chapel Hill as possible and had her own family. They would always be able to find her. They would always be able to *see* her, wherever she was.

'I respect you,' Kristina protested, and Gemma got a sudden strangled feeling, as if a hand were closing around her throat. Her father was twelve years older than Kristina. He and his twin brother, Ted, had both been to West Point, like their father before them. Geoffrey had gone on

to become a military strategist, and he never let anyone –
least of all Gemma and her mom – forget it. *Respect.* That
was the drumbeat of their lives. *Respect.* He could write
a book, she thought, about respect, and discipline, and
order, and work. He could probably write a whole *series.*

On the other hand, what he knew about *acceptance* and
*tolerance* and *his own daughter* would barely fill up a tweet.

Sometimes Gemma wondered how it was possible they
were made from the same genetic material. Her father
was angular and cold everywhere she was warm and soft
and sensitive. But the proof was there. She would have
so much rather looked like her mother. Instead she had
her father's hazel eyes, his square chin, his way of smiling
with the corners of his mouth turned down, as if neither
of them had ever quite learned to do it correctly.

'I didn't want to worry you,' Gemma's mom went on.
'Gemma said it was just a prank. Some girls have been
giving her a hard time at school, and –'

'A prank, Kristina? Are you blind? This wasn't a prank.
This was a message. Do you know who Frankenstein is?'

'Of course I know –'

'Frankenstein is the *doctor.* In the original story, in the
real version, he's the one who made the monster.' There
was a long moment of silence. Gemma could feel her
heart beating painfully, swollen like a bruise. 'This was a
message for me.'

*He's the one who made the monster.*

*This was a message for me.*

She tried to love her father. She tried to believe he loved her, as Kristina insisted that he did. She had made excuses, the same ones her mom always parroted back to her. *He's bad at expressing feelings. He's stressed at work. He didn't get a lot of love from his father.*

But deep, deep down, Gemma had always suspected that the reason her father avoided her, the reason he could barely look her in the eye, the reason he kept all her baby pictures locked up in drawers and desks instead of proudly on display in frames, the reason he could hardly speak to her without losing his temper, as if she were always paying for a crime she didn't know she had committed, was much simpler.

He couldn't stand her.

He thought she was a disappointment. A defective model, but one, sadly, that couldn't be exchanged or returned.

Her mother said something else, something Gemma didn't hear. There was a high whining in her ears, as if they were filled with bees. She wanted to turn around and run, to flee back to her bedroom, to wake and realize this had all been a dream. But she couldn't move.

'There was a breach at Haven,' her father said.

'What do you mean, *breach*?'

'Apparently, one of them escaped,' Geoff said.

A long pause. 'Well, it won't live. No way can it live. The currents on that island . . .'

'But what if it does? Jesus Christ, Kristina. Can you imagine? Can you imagine the absolute shitstorm if the story gets out? We'll be persecuted. We'll be *executed*.'

Kristina's voice rose in pitch. 'No one will know what we've done,' she says. 'How *could* they?'

Her father barked out a laugh – an angry, bitter sound. 'There are ways, trust me. All you have to do is follow the money.'

'But you left Fine and Ives for that reason. You *refused* to participate –'

'Too little, too late. I knew what Saperstein was planning. I knew where the new round of funding would go.'

Gemma could no longer follow the thread of the conversation. Still, she remained motionless, gripping the banister, trying to squeeze down a mounting scream. She could see her mother worrying the hem of her bathrobe between her fingers, and her father pacing, passing in and out of view. The angle made it impossible to see his face – a small blessing.

After a while, he spoke again. 'Bowling Springs is only fifty miles from Haven.'

Gemma's mother looked up. Her face was very pale, her eyes like two holes. 'No,' she said. Gemma was shocked.

She'd never heard her mother say no to her father. 'You can't. Gemma's been looking forward to this trip for ages. *April* has been looking forward to it. What will I tell her moms?'

'I don't care what you tell them,' he said. 'It isn't safe. Not after what happened today. Fifty miles, Kristina.'

Gemma felt as if her chest had been filled with wet concrete. She couldn't breathe.

'Oh, Geoff. Fifty miles is a lot. You can't really believe –'

'I don't *believe*, Kristina. I know.' He rounded on her, and Kristina drew backward several inches. Gemma felt a sudden wave of hatred toward him, stronger than anything she'd ever felt. For one awful second, she wished for him to die, struck down by an invisible force. But that was too cruel. She wished instead that he would simply vanish. *Blip.* As if he'd never existed at all. 'Those *nutcases* have been swarming the beach for months. Last week, they attacked one of the orderlies on her way to the ferry.'

'But you said yourself they're nutcases,' Kristina says. 'No one actually *believes* them. Besides, they don't know anything. Half of them think Haven is home to vampires, for God's sake. They'll get tired soon enough and find another cause. And what does that have to do with Gemma? No one could possibly know –'

'Someone *does* know,' he said, cutting her off. 'That's

the point. I'm not sending her into the middle of that mess. She can go on spring break next year.'

Gemma opened her mouth and let out a long, silent scream. She imagined the sound shattering the chandelier, blowing out the windows, exploding all of her father's priceless porcelain antiques.

'Fine.' Kristina stood up, swaying a little on her feet. Gemma couldn't tell if it was the lingering effects of the sleeping pills, or because of the physical effort of standing up to the great Geoffrey Ives. 'But *you* have to be the one to tell her. It'll break her heart, and I won't do it.'

'Fine,' her father said, and then, to Gemma's horror, he flung open the door and stomped into the foyer.

She turned quickly and slipped down the hall again, her heart beating out the word *unfair, unfair.* In her room, she shoved Rufus aside and climbed under the covers, mounding a pillow over her head as if it could smother the sounds of what she had just heard. She waited, tight with anxiety, to hear her father's footsteps outside her door. How would she face him now? How would she face him ever again?

But minutes passed, and he didn't come, and slowly the tension in her body dissipated, replaced by the heavy sensation of lying at the very bottom of a pit. She was filled with a gnawing sense of injustice, of anger, of flat-out grief. *Unfair.* She didn't understand half of what her parents had said. All she knew was that yet again, she was trapped. *Unfair.* She was like an insect in her father's hand; maybe he got pleasure just from squeezing, from watching her squirm.

She didn't think she would ever fall asleep again. But she did, eventually, hours later, when the light in her room had turned the color of dark chalk. And when she woke up, her father had been called away to Shanghai on business, and so it was Gemma's mother who broke the news after all.

# FOUR

SHE DIDN'T GO TO SCHOOL on Friday, claiming she was sick, and her mom didn't even bug her about what was wrong – a sure sign she knew Gemma was faking.

Gemma was glad her dad was once again traveling. Glad they were separated by time zones and a big ocean. She couldn't have faced him. If she had, she thought she would have spit at him, or kicked him in the shins, or finally said some of the things she'd been meaning to say for sixteen years.

The great Geoffrey Ives, cofounder of Fine & Ives Pharmaceuticals, Master of the Universe, *total fucking asshole.*

April called her during homeroom, a useless fifteen minutes of time between second and third periods when random juniors got shuffled together to suffer through announcements about basketball games, prom, and Tolerance Week.

After the third time Gemma didn't pick up, April resorted to texting, flooding Gemma's phone with scowling selfies. *What the shit is going on?? Are you okay?*

Gemma felt a sudden surge of viciousness, a desire to cause pain, since she had been caused pain. Maybe this was how Chloe and the wolves felt: maybe somewhere deep in their lives, someone was nipping at them, trying to make them bleed. *No,* she wrote back. Then: *not going tomorrow.*

There was a five-minute space between messages. Gemma wasn't sure whether April was stunned or just pretending to pay attention to her homeroom teacher.

Her next message said: *This is a joke, right?*

She could have written back, explaining. Better yet, she could have called. She could already imagine April shoving the phone deep into her pocket while she hurried into the nearest bathroom stall, then perching, knees to chest, on a toilet seat and pressing the phone to her ear while Gemma sobbed. She could have explained about the broken window, and her father's terrible words: *This was a message for me. . . .* It had all come true: her crashing fears, the strange terrors that had always infected her. Her father hated her. She might someday leave, but she would never escape – not him, not that truth, not really.

But she had already cried – had woken, in fact, with

her throat raw and the taste of salt on her lips, and realized she'd been crying in her sleep – and today she felt nothing but a strange, bobbing sense of emptiness, as if she was a balloon untethered from the earth, slowly floating away into nothingness. She wondered whether her mom felt this way when she took pills.

So she wrote back: *not a joke.*

And, after a minute: *sorry.*

Her phone stayed quiet after that.

For the first two days of spring break, Gemma did nothing. She watched TV on her computer without knowing what she was watching. She slumped from upstairs to downstairs to microwave food her dad wouldn't have approved of her eating, the Hot Pockets and frozen mac and cheese she'd convinced Bernice, their housekeeper, to buy for her, Chinese takeout that had mysteriously materialized in the fridge. Once she took Rufus to the backyard and stood in her pajamas, blinking in the sun, while he ran circles around Danny, one of the lawn guys (she thought that was his name, anyway; there had been so many), who was moving slowly on the enormous lawn mower like a ship captain through a sea of green.

Her mom, who would normally have peppered Gemma with constant questions, or asked that she come have lunch at the club, or suggested they do mani-pedis

– all activities that Gemma hated – largely left her alone. They were like two snowflakes, drifting through the vast white house, encased in their own arrangements of pain and misery.

All, she thought, her father's fault: her father's rules. Her father's house. Her father's walls, white and oversized, made pretty with ornate picture frames and chandeliers, so pretty they might keep a person from knowing she was trapped. Even, she realized, her father's pills. She'd never before thought about the fact that her dad's old company probably manufactured the meds her mother took, day in and day out, to help her sleep or wake or keep her from dreaming.

If she was honest, she realized that some small part of her – okay, maybe a big part of her – had been hoping that because she wasn't going to Florida, April wouldn't go. And she knew that if she'd told April the truth, April wouldn't have gone: she would have gladly spent spring break watching bad TV or trying to learn the choreography of stupid pop videos from YouTube. It was her fault, which made her feel mean and stupid and small. But the fact that April *did* go made her feel mean and stupid and small – and also abandoned.

She was wallowing, and she was pretty deep.

On the third day of spring break, Gemma woke up and felt a desperate, urgent desire to move, to *do* something.

April had been at her grandparents' house for a full thirty-six hours. Gemma knew this because, in a moment of true, epic pathetic-ness, she had logged onto April's iTunes account and used Find My Phone to track April's progress down the coast – they had traded passwords years ago so they could always find each other if they were ever separated in a zombie apocalypse, assuming Wi-Fi still worked. No doubt April was already working on her tan and trying to scope out cute guys to flirt with who didn't know she was an alien.

Gemma knew by now April would have heard about the Frankenstein mask, or at least some version of the story filtered through their parents, and Gemma wished they could talk about it. Why had the mask freaked her father out so badly? She wished she'd been listening more carefully to her parents' midnight conversation. Already, the conversation seemed like a dream. She couldn't remember details, just a place called Haven, a word she thought she remembered vaguely from childhood. A hospital, maybe? One of the boards her father sat on? He consulted for dozens of companies, all with names like NeoTech and Amalgam and Complete Solutions.

Missing April was like having a hole in the very bottom of her stomach. Like period cramps, as if she was puffy and swollen and bruised but on the inside. Gemma wasn't gay, she didn't think (although she didn't know, having never kissed anything but a practice pillow – and in a moment of complete, delirious silliness, given one practice blow job on a cucumber), but that didn't stop her from being stupid in love with her best friend.

She sent a picture of one of her oldest stuffed animals, an octopus missing two legs thanks to Rufus's rabid appetite for anything stuffed. He was April's favorite. *I miss you! Hope you're having fun!* she'd written, and then left her phone in her bed, buried under a pillow, in case April was still mad and didn't write back. Besides, she didn't want her mom calling her every five seconds.

Leaving the house wasn't a problem. It was early, and her mom was probably at her spin class. Leaving the *property* was a slightly bigger problem, since she a) had no car, and b) had never even learned to drive. She leashed up Rufus. It was a shortish walk down the drive, past Danny, who was pruning the hedges today, out the gates, and to the bus that ran past the university down to Franklin Street, with its pretty clutter of bars and cafés and the college bookstore selling UNC gear. Rufus loved the bus and sat the whole time on the seat next to Gemma, like a person, with his nose pressed against the window.

It was a beautiful day. She wandered down Franklin, looking in shop windows, debating whether to buy something. The town felt emptier than usual: UNC students were on spring break, too, until Monday. She kept picturing the phantoms of all her classmates, flitting by her on empty streets, while their real selves were four hundred miles away, lathering on sunscreen or taking tequila shots at breakfast.

She had just turned onto Rosemary Street, half thinking she would stop in at Mama Dip's for hush puppies even though she wasn't hungry, when she got a sudden nervous feeling in her stomach, as if she'd approached the edge of a cliff unexpectedly.

Watched. She was being watched.

If she'd been alone, in the dark, she might have been too afraid to turn around. But she was standing between the orthodontist's office where she'd had her braces tightened for three years and a small Mobil station that sold postcards touting North Carolina's many beauties. So she turned, even as the sense of dread yawned open wider, like a mouth lodged beneath her ribs.

She relaxed. No one. An older guy muttering about a parking ticket wedged under his windshield, a group of women – two of them she recognized as her mom's yoga friends – standing outside Mama Dip's. Patti Winters, the mother of a hideous girl in Gemma's grade whose endless bids for popularity meant she treated Gemma like the weakling who had to be eaten so the tribe could flourish, looked up and caught sight of Gemma. She waved and started to cross the street to come over.

Quickly, Gemma turned around, pretending not to have seen, and hurried across the gas station parking lot. She tied Rufus up to the sign that indicated a handicapped parking space and slipped inside the Quick-Mart, darting behind a display of cheap plastic sunglasses. Pete Rogers, aka Perv Rogers (a nickname assigned to him in third grade, when on a class trip he'd been caught stealing a pair of underwear from Chloe's overnight bag), eyed her from behind the register.

After fifteen seconds, Gemma felt like an idiot, and once again, missed April badly. She was still in school mode, prey mode. A rabbit on the run. But her mom's friends weren't going to track her and pin her down with conversation about why she was home on spring break and where-were-all-her-friends. She bought a heart-shaped pair of red sunglasses, because she didn't want to seem like she was hiding, which of course she was.

'I like your style,' Perv said, in a pervy way. Gemma frowned at him.

No one was waiting for her in the parking lot. Patti Winters was long gone. Rufus was lying on the pavement, tongue out in the heat.

Still, as she began crossing with him back toward the street, she got that nervous, alert feeling again, as if someone were whispering something mean just a little too softly for her to hear. The guy who'd gotten the parking ticket was now refueling, his shitty old Chevrolet pulled haphazardly up to the pump. Their eyes met briefly, and he opened his mouth, as if to say something to her.

She was almost passing him, and that was when her brain click-clicked into motion, and gears slotted together, and she realized all at once that he wasn't getting gas – his car wasn't even connected to the pump – and he hadn't just randomly looked at her. He'd been watching her.

He was following her.

But by the time she understood this, they had drawn level. He grabbed her wrist and pulled, a motion seamless and small and effective, so she dropped Rufus's leash. Rufus just stood there patiently, wagging his tail. Gemma was too shocked to cry out, but then she was pinned to the man, temporarily so close she could see the wide black expanse of pores freckled across his nose, the sweat beading on his upper lip.

'Gem,' he said. His breath smelled like coffee and like old, moldy closets. His hair was long and looked unwashed. 'Listen to me. I don't want any trouble.'

Her mind moved in short, explosive bursts, sending up disconnected images and ideas. She must know him. How else would he know her name? She searched his face, lean and cavernous, pitted with old acne scars and covered all over with stubble, and the taste of acid burned her throat as her brain made a final winding *click-click*.

Abducted. She was being abducted.

More lightning flashes in her brain: ransom demands; a cold, wet basement fitted with chains and old torture devices.

He fumbled the door open with one hand, keeping a grip on her wrist with the other. 'I'm not going to hurt you, okay?' He was panting hard. 'You gotta trust me. We're gonna be okay.' As if they were on the same side.

She got a quick glimpse of a backseat littered with empty soda cans and crumpled receipts, a baseball hat, plastic bags from Party City, a dark thatch of something that looked like a huge, furry spider, and at that moment she found her voice and screamed. Or she tried to scream. What came out was more of a hoarse shout. Even her vocal cords were shaking, petrified. Only then did Rufus begin to bark.

The man instantly released her, springing backward, pressing himself against the car as if she'd just whipped out a weapon.

'Jesus.' He was shouting now too, angrily. 'Jesus. Why'd you go and do that, huh?'

She turned, snatched up Rufus's leash, and ran. It had been so long since she'd run — since she was allowed to run — she was worried her legs wouldn't work. But they did. She careened back toward the Quick-Mart, her heart exploding through her ribs, nearly toppling an old woman who'd just emerged, holding a fistful of lottery tickets. She didn't bother tying Rufus up. She wanted him next to her, anyway, even though he was evidently the world's worst guard dog.

'What do you know about heaven?' the man shouted to her, or at least she thought he did. By the time she was inside, taking deep, hiccuping breaths of air standing beside the windows papered over with flyers advertising deals on milk and Bud Light and cigarettes, he was gone.

'You're not supposed to have dogs in here,' Perv said. 'Sorry. State law.'

Gemma ignored that. 'Can I borrow your phone?' No way was she getting back on the bus. She had an itchy, exposed feeling, even standing in the warm, familiar must of the Quick-Mart. She wanted to go to the bathroom and scrub off her wrist, where the man had grabbed her.

'Are you okay?' he asked, squinting at her. 'You look really –'

She glared at him. Fortunately, he shut up. She punched in her mother's number, her fingers shaking so badly she fumbled it the first time.

'Gemma? Gemma, what's the matter?' she said, as soon as Gemma choked out a hello. 'Where are you? Whose number is this?'

She almost lost it and started to cry. But Perv was still watching her – he wasn't actually bad-looking, with very clear skin and straight teeth and messy blond hair that looked as if he'd just had his head out the window of a moving car – so she kept it together.

'I'm okay,' she said. 'I – I missed the bus. And I'm not feeling well.'

She'd said the magic words: *not feeling well.* Her mom's tone instantly changed. She became brisk, businesslike, as she always was about her daughter's health.

'I'm coming,' she said. 'Where?'

Gemma explained and hung up, passing the phone back to Perv and scowling at him so he would know not to ask questions. As soon as her mom came, she would tell her everything. She wished now she'd paid more attention to the car – it was a white Chevrolet, she knew, and old, but she hadn't caught even one digit of the license plate. Jesus. She'd always thought she would be good in a crisis: cool, ironic, detached. But her knees were shaking. She hadn't picked up even one good detail they could tell the police, except that the guy liked McDonald's. That narrowed it down to a bazillion people.

It took her mom fifteen minutes to get there, and Gemma spent the whole time ignoring Perv's looks of concern, trying to keep Rufus from going after the display of beef jerky, and doing her best to recall every single detail of the man's interaction with her. And by the time her mom pulled up – leaving the BMW door open as she jogged out of the car, still in yoga pants, scanning the parking lot for Gemma as though she expected her to be curled up in a fetal position on the ground – and then gripped both of Gemma's shoulders and demanded to know what was wrong, what had happened, Gemma only smiled tightly.

'I got tired,' she said. She knew she probably looked like shit and wouldn't have to fake it. 'I did too much walking, I think.'

Because by then her mind, grinding slowly through its memory spool, had glitched on a few small details that in retrospect became huge, all-important: the shopping bags from Party City, which sold Halloween masks – like Frankenstein's – year-round. The fact that he'd called her Gem.

More importantly, the last thing he'd said to her, which in memory became clarified, distilled, amplified. Not: *What do you know about heaven?*

But: *What do you know about Haven?*

# FIVE

GEMMA WASN'T ACTUALLY EXPECTING TO find much of anything by Googling Haven. She thought she'd heard her parents talk about Haven before, although other than their fight of the previous week she couldn't remember specific instances of it.

The first time she typed in the search term, she got back a random assortment of articles and web pages: a band named Haven was releasing its fourth studio album; a woman named Debbie Haven had recently been convicted of seducing one of her teenage students; a bioethicist named Richard Haven, founder of a famous research institute, had driven his car off the road in Florida the same year Gemma was born; the same Richard Haven had left a large sum of money in his will to the University of Pennsylvania, where for years he had been a professor emeritus. Nothing that pertained to her, nothing that made sense. She felt almost relieved.

But then she had the idea to type in Haven plus her last name, Ives.

Instantly, there were over a million results, all of them pertaining to the Haven Institute – Gemma quickly realized this must be the same research facility founded by Richard Haven – located on Spruce Island, somewhere off the coast of Florida. She found a PDF credited to her father's old company, Fine & Ives Pharmaceuticals. In it, a letter to the shareholders, the board wrote of hiring Haven to perform the company's research and development. But it was dated several years *after* her father had ruptured with the cofounder of the company and been ousted from the board.

She kept clicking and eventually turned up a picture of her father, standing at some kind of a gala next to a blond guy who looked like he belonged in a commercial for surf gear but who was, according to the caption, the famous Richard Haven. Next to them was a man with a dark curling beard and a forehead, sharply angled, that gave him the look of a shark: Dr. Mark Saperstein, a name that again registered very dimly with her from childhood. She remembered that her father had mentioned Saperstein the other night. *I knew what Saperstein was planning.* A quick Google search revealed that Saperstein had replaced Richard Haven after his death at the institute that bore his name.

She kept toggling through results, increasingly con-fused. If Fine & Ives hadn't contracted Haven for its research until well after her father left, why were there so many photos of him getting chummy with Richard Haven? She found an interview with Haven himself for the Scientific Medical Association, crediting her father for his 'tireless support of medical research and advances in stem-cell technology.'

She resumed her search, this time typing in *Haven Insti-tute*. The official website was one of those bland templates that all research facilities seemed to share, filled with yawningly boring terminology like *neurobiological resolution* and *cutting-edge biotech services*. She found nothing listed on the website to indicate what kind of research Haven did, exactly — at least nothing she could understand. The insti-tute, she noted, had been opened the year before she was born. Whatever her father felt about Haven now, Haven couldn't have been the reason he'd left Fine & Ives. The timing wasn't right.

More interesting were the websites about Haven: mil-lions of results, half of them blogs, conspiracy websites, and speculative articles about what really went on there, what kind of research was performed, and whether any of it was legal. Some articles were straight-up sci-fi, and claimed that the island was a place where hybrid animals were being manufactured for military use, or where aliens were being studied and even trained. Other bloggers speculated that at Haven scientists performed illegal stem-cell research.

One of the websites cited most frequently was called HavenFiles.com. When she clicked over to it, a bright-orange warning, exuberantly punctuated and capitalized, flashed at the top of the screen.

*Don't be fooled by phony websites and reports!!* it said. *Haven-Files.com is the NUMBER ONE source for TRUTHFUL and VERIFIED reporting on the Haven Institute!!*

Half-amused, half-curious, she began to read. The website was, as far as she could tell, operated by some guy down in Florida named Jacob Witz, who had, for whatever reason, dedicated his life to reporting on various theories, rumors, and phenomena pertaining to Haven. His bio showed a picture of a gap-toothed middle-aged guy squinting into the sun, wearing a fishing hat feathered with different lures. He looked exactly like the kind of person you'd expect to see tipsy and railing about the time he was abducted by aliens. In his bio, half treatise, half manifesto, he revealed that he'd been a journalism major at the University of Miami and that he was devoted to 'integrity,' 'uncovering the facts about one of the military's best-kept SECRETS,' and 'delivering KNOWLEDGE to the AMERICAN PUBLIC in accordance with the tenets of FREE SPEECH.' This last sentence was punctuated with about forty exclamation points.

'All right, crazy,' Gemma said out loud. 'Let's see what you got.'

His website was like one of those all-you-can-eat buffets where food keeps getting replenished, no matter how much you load up: every page led to more and more pages, every link to more and more links. Gemma felt as if she were falling down a well. There were detailed maps of Haven as imagined from above, and blurry pictures of the buildings taken from a distance and obviously from some sort of boat. (Reading between the lines, Gemma felt sure that Witz had never actually set foot on the island, which was guarded by troops and enclosed within a jail-style fence. He had pictures of this, too, dreary chain-link fitted with barbed wire that Gemma estimated to be about sixteen feet high.) Dozens of pages were devoted to the various theories about the experimentation done at Haven, and Witz argued carefully, in great detail, against the idea that Haven was manufacturing monsters or performing tests on aliens – although he was quick to say that he was an 'expert' in military cover-ups of alien landings and had even written a self-published book on the subject (*The Secret Others: What the US Government Doesn't Want You to Know!*).

Several whole pages were devoted to something called the 'Nurse M controversy': Nurse M, real name unknown, who supposedly committed suicide after working at Haven, the day before Witz, who had tracked her down but at least on the site refused to reveal her real name, was supposed to interview her. She found a link to a three-year-old news story in which Haven was named, supposedly because a nationwide hospital system was illegally selling off embryonic and fetal cells to research facilities. An embedded video showed one of the hospital execs leaving a courtroom, swarmed by reporters and right-to-life protesters holding graphic handmade signs.

Gemma's back was sore and her eyes burned from staring at the screen. She was shocked to see she'd been at it for three hours already. Still, she had more questions than she had answers. Her father's company had contracted Haven to do research and development for them. So what? Fine & Ives was one of the largest pharmaceutical companies in the country. They contracted plenty of research facilities – and besides, her father had already left by that point, after a protracted court battle with his former partner.

Why did the man in the parking lot think she'd know anything about Haven? And why was it important in the first place? What *did* go on at Haven? Why all the secrecy, and the guards, and that fence?

There was something she was missing, something obvious and yet hidden, like one of those visual riddles where a picture can be viewed two different ways. She wished she could get into her father's office, but he of course kept the door locked. Besides, she didn't even know what she was supposed to be looking for.

She stood up, did a clumsy approximation of a yoga stretch, and nearly fell over. Rufus raised his head and blinked at her.

'So much for Zen,' she said. Obviously unimpressed, Rufus flopped back onto her pillow.

Almost instantly, the buzzer sounded downstairs. Someone was at the gate. Rufus sprang to his feet and dove off the bed, barking furiously, charging for the stairs. For a second, Gemma worried it might be Chloe again, maybe back to do a second round of damage.

But that was stupid. Chloe wouldn't bother buzzing – besides, she was probably on spring break getting trashed on cheap tequila shots with the rest of her pack wolves. And though she'd been certain only a few days ago that Chloe had been the one to throw the Frankenstein mask, now she was having doubts. Maybe, if all the rumors about Haven and monsters were true, it really had been a message for her dad, even if she still couldn't understand the connection.

She checked the security camera and was surprised to

see Perv Rogers, leaning half out of the car, the shock of his white-blond hair visible despite the low resolution. But she buzzed him in without asking him what he wanted. Perv was harmless. Well, except for being a pervert and maybe keeping girls' underwear strung around his basement for sniffing. Maybe keeping *girls* in his basement.

Rufus was still barking two minutes later, when Perv's car – a purplish minivan that looked like a giant, mobile eggplant, obviously borrowed from one of his parents – came rolling up the drive. She had to hold Rufus by his collar so he didn't bolt into the front yard.

'Sorry,' she said, over the sounds of his continued barking, even as Perv climbed out of the car and began edging cautiously toward the door. 'He doesn't bite, I promise. He just likes to make a lot of noise. Sit down, Rufus.' Rufus finally sat, and even licked Perv's hand when Perv bent down and presented it for sniffing.

'How old is he?' Perv asked.

'An artifact,' Gemma said. 'Thirteen. But still really healthy,' she added quickly, because she had a superstition about referring to Rufus's age. He'd arrived as a puppy when she was three years old. She had no memories that didn't include him.

'I probably smell like Quick-Mart hot dogs,' Perv said. He must have changed after work, because instead of his crappy collared shirt he was actually dressed nicely, in a white button-down that showed off skin that was half tan and half just freckly, plus a pair of faded chino shorts and old Chuck Taylors. She realized she was wearing an old Hannah Montana T-shirt – *ironically*, of course, but he wouldn't know that – and crossed her arms over her chest.

'What are you doing here?' she asked.

'You forgot your change,' he said, digging into one pocket and producing a few crumpled bills and some loose change. 'There you go. Three dollars and twenty-seven cents.'

She stared at him. 'You drove to my house to give me three dollars?'

'And twenty-seven cents,' he repeated, smiling broadly. 'Besides, I wanted to see where you live. I heard your house was kind of awesome.' He craned his neck, looking beyond her into the house. 'Oh, man. Is that a chandelier? I thought chandeliers were for hotels and Las Vegas casinos. And maybe Mexican drug lords.'

'Are you serious?' Gemma had maybe spoken three words to Perv in her whole life before their exchange in the Quick-Mart – most recently *no*, when he'd turned around in bio and asked whether she knew that in sea horses, only the male carried the eggs.

'Sorry.' Perv rubbed a hand over his hair, making it stick up, flame-like. 'Sometimes my mouth says things without checking in with my brain first.'

'Yeah, I get that,' Gemma said. 'Mexican drug lords?'
Perv shrugged. He seemed to be waiting for something,
but she had no idea what. He was the first boy who'd
ever come over to see her – not that he was there to see
*her*, really – and she was suddenly mortified. She wanted
Perv to leave, but didn't know how to ask without seem-
ing mean. After all, he'd just done her a favor. And he
was nice, even if he did steal girls' underwear. And possibly, you know, have a sex chamber in his basement, as
April had once theorized when she caught Perv staring at
Gemma in the cafeteria.

'So can I?' Perv asked, after looking at her patiently
for a bit.

'Can you what?'

He blinked. 'Come in and see where you live.'

She didn't want to say yes but couldn't think of a way
to refuse. So she shuffled backward, taking Rufus by the
collar. 'Okay,' she said. 'I mean, if you really want.'

Perv took a step forward and then hesitated. 'You
sure that thing doesn't like the taste of human flesh?' He
pointed at Rufus.

She rolled her eyes. 'Please. He's a grumpy old man.
He likes to make a lot of noise, especially around people
he doesn't –' She broke off suddenly. She'd just remembered that Rufus, who still barked as if the world was
ending whenever a stranger came to the door, hadn't

made a sound when the man had approached her in the parking lot, at least not until Gemma shouted. He'd even wagged his tail. Almost as if . . .

Almost as if he recognized the man, knew him from somewhere.

She was gripped, then, by a terrible feeling: that something was coming. Something she couldn't understand. The man, Haven, her father – all of it was tangled up together, and she, Gemma, was at the center of the mess, the heart of the shitstorm.

Head shit.

Perv was still prattling on, oblivious. 'Damn. Is that your mom in the oil painting?'

'It's a watercolor,' Gemma said automatically.

'Wow. Cool. Your mom's kind of hot. Is that weird?'

'Yes.' Gemma's head hurt. 'Listen, I'm really sorry. But I'm kinda not feeling great. It's not really a good time for me. . . .'

But he didn't seem to hear. He'd just spotted the bathroom off the foyer. 'Holy shit. Is that a TV? Right next to the toilet?' He disappeared, although she could still hear him talking, his voice tinny and distorted by the tile. He reemerged a second later, midsentence. '. . . snorkel in that bathtub. It's like the spring break of shower models.'

Gemma took a deep breath. 'Has anyone ever told you that you talk a lot?'

'All the time,' Perv said, grinning. 'It's kind of my trademark. So, what else you got? A hidden bowling alley? An indoor pool?'

'No bowling alley,' she said. She was tempted to add: *And the pool's out back.* But that would only encourage him. 'Listen, seriously, can we rain check on the tour?' She said it knowing a rain check was unlikely. It wasn't as if she and Perv were friends. Sure, he'd always been nice to her – he never laughed when someone whispered about one of her scars, for example, or called her *Frankenstein* – but he was pretty much nice to everybody. He was probably one of those do-gooder, Save-the-Manatees types. Maybe he thought being nice to Gemma would win him karmic brownie points.

'Sure,' he said. He did a semi-decent job of concealing his disappointment. 'I should get home anyway. I'm leaving for Florida tomorrow, and my mom's acting like I'm heading off to war. I swear, there may be a twelve-salute send-off.'

Florida. The word set off little sparks in Gemma's mind. 'Where in Florida?' she asked, trying to sound casual.

He'd already started for the door. Now he turned around, shrugging. 'Tallent Hill,' he said. 'No one's ever heard of it. It's like an hour outside of Tampa.'

'I've heard of it,' Gemma said quickly. And she

had – Tallent Hill was just outside the Chassahowitzka National Wildlife Refuge, a little more than an hour south of Barrel Key, where boats carrying staff and supplies to and from Haven launched. She remembered seeing Tallent Hill on one of the detailed maps on the Haven Files website.

With a sudden, electric sense of clarity, she knew: she had to get to Florida. She had to go there, to Haven, and see it for herself.

'My aunt has a time-share there,' he was saying. 'And she makes a killer margarita. Alcohol free, but still. What's spring break without relatives and cocktails, right?' He shoved his hands in his pockets. 'What about you? You got any big plans?'

'Actually' – Gemma licked her lips; her mouth was suddenly dry – 'I was supposed to be driving down to Florida. To Barrel Key.'

Perv raised his eyebrows but said nothing.

She kept going, elaborating on the lie as she went, hoping he couldn't see how badly she was blushing. 'There was a problem with my car' – a clumsy lie; there were three cars in the driveway alone, but whatever, he wouldn't know the difference – 'and now I'm kind of stranded. I was thinking of taking a Greyhound . . . ?' She trailed off hopefully.

'No,' he said immediately. 'No way. I once got stranded

on a Greyhound for nine hours with nothing to eat but a pack of Tic Tacs. *And* the toilet backed up. Friends don't let friends take the bus.'

Gemma raised her eyebrows. 'So we're friends now?'

'Sure we are,' he said, reaching out and chucking her gently on the arm. When he took a step forward, she could smell him. He didn't smell like hot dogs at all, but like something clean and also a little bit spicy. 'We became friends when we agreed to take a road trip. I'll pick you up at nine tomorrow.'

April screamed when she found out that Gemma was coming down to Florida after all – Gemma had to yank the phone away from her ear to avoid having her eardrums blown out. April was so excited, she didn't even ask Gemma how she was planning to make the trip – thankfully, since Gemma thought she might die if she had to admit Perv Rogers was going to drive her.

'I don't believe it,' she said. Their fight had been completely forgotten. 'Gemma Ives. I didn't know you had it in you. And your parents just caved?'

'I guess they were done playing bad cop,' Gemma said. Lying gave her a sticky feeling in her chest, like she'd accidentally inhaled a condom. Fortunately, her father's business trip would keep him in Shanghai for at least the next week, so that left only Kristina to deceive. Still,

Gemma had no idea how she would deal with lying to her mom – and not just lying, but sneaking off to a different state.

She wasn't exactly a natural rebel. The one time she and April had decided sophomore year to try an e-cigarette, Gemma had been so terrified the next day that she was dying of cancer that she had confessed to her mom just so she could be reassured.

But at eight a.m. the next morning Kristina would be in a long board meeting of one of the charities she supported, which meant that Gemma had a solid four hours to get the hell out of the state before her mom even found out she was missing.

Kristina and Gemma ate in front of the TV that night, side by side, as they often did whenever Gemma's dad was traveling. Usually, their game was to turn on a trashy reality television show and make fun of all the contestants. But tonight, Gemma was too antsy and distracted to concentrate.

'Can you believe her lips?' Kristina said, gesturing with a fork at the TV. 'It looks like she got attacked by a vacuum cleaner.' Gemma laughed, but a second too late. Kristina turned to her. 'Are you all right? You seem quiet.' Then, alarmed: 'Are you feeling okay?'

'I'm fine,' Gemma said. She set down her dinner – takeout from Whole Foods, since her mom considered *cooking* selecting from the various prepared options – on the coffee table and nudged it away from Rufus's nose with a toe. The sticky feeling was still lodged in her chest. Without meaning to, she blurted out, 'Why did Dad leave Fine and Ives?'

Kristina turned to her, obviously startled. For a second, she looked almost afraid. Then she became immediately suspicious. 'Why are you asking?'

Gemma shrugged. 'Just curious. I mean, it was his, wasn't it? It still has his name and everything. I was so little. . . .' Gemma was two when her dad had first decided to leave Fine & Ives, but the subsequent lawsuit had dragged on for more than three years. She remembered nothing about that time; her childhood memories consisted mostly of hospital visits, doctors and constant evaluations, illnesses, relapses, injections, and bitter medicine spooned to her by her mother. But she did remember her parents had celebrated the end of the lawsuit in her room at Duke University Hospital, and she remembered being overwhelmed with happiness and with a sense even then that it wouldn't last. It never lasted.

Kristina turned back to the TV. But she was no lon ger watching. That was obvious. And after a second she picked up the remote and clicked the mute button. 'Your father and Matthew Fine had . . . disagreements about the company's direction.'

'What kind of disagreements?' Gemma pressed.

Kristina sighed. 'To be honest, Gem, the details were never clear even to me.' She said the words lightly, and Gemma knew they'd been practiced before. 'Matthew Fine wanted to make some investments and your father disagreed. It was all boring and very, very complicated.' Kristina's eyelids flickered: a sure sign that she was lying.

Gemma thought that would be the end of that, but then Kristina turned to her.

'I know your dad can be difficult,' she said, making a weird face, as if the words were sour. 'He's made his mistakes, like everyone. But he's a good man. Deep down, he is.'

Gemma nearly said, *If you say so*. But she swallowed back the words. No point in getting into an argument with her mom – not when, if everything went according to plan, there were so many arguments in her future.

# SIX

GEMMA WAS ABSOLUTELY SURE THAT something would go wrong. Kristina would know something was the matter and refuse to go to her board meeting. Perv would show up at nine and the truth would come out and Gemma would be locked in her room until menopause.

She was a nervous wreck. She couldn't imagine how thieves and murderers kept their cool. She could barely sneak out without her stomach liquefying.

But her mom just kissed Gemma's cheek, as she always did, and promised to be home later for another Whole Foods and reality TV marathon. One good thing about being relatively friendless and a total Goody Two-shoes: no one ever expected you to do anything wrong. Gemma was suspicion-proof.

She packed her bag, unpacked it, realized she'd packed all the wrong things and far too many of them, and repacked. She was too nervous to sit at her laptop, although she did pull up the Haven Files again on her phone and swipe through the maps section, partially to reassure herself of its existence.

Perv showed up punctually, driving the same eggplant-colored minivan. This time, Rufus hauled himself to the door but let out only three restrained barks of welcome.

'Bye, Roo.' Gemma knelt down to hug her dog, taking comfort in his familiar smell. She knew she was being ridiculous – she was only going to be gone for a few days, maybe less if her mom got really aggressive and decided to fly down to Florida to get her – but she couldn't help but feel she was leaving forever. And she was, in a sense. She was leaving her old self behind. She would no longer be Gemma-who-did-everything-right, who-listened-to-her-parents, Fragile Gemma of the Broken Body. She was Gemma-who-rode-with-strange-boys, Gemma-who-investigated-mysteries, Gemma-who-defied-parents-and-lied-to-best-friends.

Ninja Gemma.

'Ready to rock?' Perv asked, when she came outside with her backpack slung over one shoulder. Today he was wearing a green T-shirt that made his hair look even blonder and a pair of striped Bermuda shorts.

'Sure.' Gemma let Perv take the bag from her, though

it wasn't heavy, and sling it in the trunk. 'How long is the drive, anyway?'

'Normally? Nine hours. When I'm behind the wheel?' Perv opened the door for her before she could do it for herself. He didn't just talk quickly. He did everything quickly. If he were a comic book character, there would be little zoom-y lines drawn behind him. 'A record eight hours and forty-five minutes. That's with a standard three pee breaks. Fine. Four,' he said, when Gemma looked at him. 'But don't blame me if it throws our timing way off.'

All morning, Gemma waited for Perv to run out of things to say. She soon realized that it was a lost cause, as were her attempts to ignore him. Trying to ignore Perv was like standing in the middle of a highway, trying to ignore the eighteen-wheeler about to turn your brains into pancake batter.

A typical conversation with Perv went like this:

'Hey, check it out. A Hostess truck. Can you imagine pulling a heist on a cupcake truck? That'd be the most delicious crime ever. You'd be a national hero. One time when I was little I tried to make cupcakes by pouring pancake batter into actual cups – my mom's china, to be exact. Turns out, interestingly, that china doesn't do very well at high heat. You know what else doesn't do well at high heat? Cell phones. Remind me to tell you about the time I accidentally microwaved my phone. . . .'

And on and on and on. Occasionally, he paused expectantly and waited for Gemma to say *uh-huh* or *no way*, or fired a series of rapid questions her way in an attempt to draw her out. For the most part, she responded in as few words as possible. She was too nervous to have a normal conversation, especially with Perv. She'd never been good with strangers and she had zero experience with boys, so the combination – *boy* and *almost stranger* – meant that her tongue felt as if it was wrestling itself every time she tried to speak. She was hoping he might take the hint and suggest they listen to music, or just leave her in peace.

No such luck.

'So your dad's some big pharma guy, right?'

'Used to be.'

'I love saying the word *pharma*. Pharma. It sounds like a type of plant. Say it.'

'Do I have to?'

'Yes. I'm driving. You're here for my amusement. Humor me.'

'Pharma.'

'See? Totally a type of plant.'

They stopped just after noon at a rest stop in South Carolina that featured a Panera and a McDonald's. As they were getting out of the car, Gemma made the mistake of calling Perv *Perv* – out loud.

'Seriously?' He made a face.

'Sorry.' Gemma felt immediately guilty. Perv was nice, and secretly she'd been flattered when April caught him staring at Gemma in the cafeteria, even if it was probably only because he had dirt in his eye or something. Nobody ever stared at her except in a horrified kind of way, as if her face was a graphic image of a car accident. And Pete was *cute* – in a very messy boy kind of way, but still, undeniably cute. *And* he was giving her a ride.

Perv – *Pete* – shook his head. He didn't look mad. Just surprised and a bit disappointed. 'You really think I'd steal underwear from *Chloe*?'

Gemma tried to make a joke out of it. 'Are you saying you'd steal it from someone else?'

She was relieved when Pete – she would only think of him as Pete from now on – cracked a smile. 'Maybe,' he said, 'under the right circumstances. Like, for the good of social justice.'

'Why would stealing underwear be good for social justice?' she asked.

'Politics are complex, Gemma,' he answered solemnly, and she couldn't help but laugh.

They agreed to meet back in the car – or rather, Pete decided they should have a race to see who could get back to the car soonest, claiming he had once ordered a McDonald's meal, peed, and purchased several plastic figurines from one of the twenty-five-cent machines that always cluttered the rest stops, all within a record four minutes.

Gemma didn't like to eat in front of strangers, ever since the time in seventh grade when Chloe had made pig-snorting noises when she'd carried her tray at lunch, and half the class had joined in. Instead she followed Pete into the rest stop and scarfed a granola bar while peeing in a stall, feeling pathetic and stupid but still too embarrassed to buy what she wanted, which was a Happy Meal. She didn't feel so much like Ninja Gemma sitting with her pants around her ankles and granola bar crumbs on her bare thighs.

She made it back to the car first, and Pete emerged about thirty seconds later at a sprint, holding an enormous bag from McDonald's. He stopped when he saw her and threw up his hands dramatically, nearly losing his soda cup.

'I don't believe it,' he said. 'You beat me.' Then, unlocking the car and seeing she was empty-handed, he said, 'You're not hungry?'

'Not really,' Gemma said, even though she was. She turned away so he wouldn't see her cheeks burning.

When they climbed into the car, he plopped the McDonald's bag in her lap. She could smell the fries.

They smelled like grease and salt and heaven.

'Share mine,' he said. 'I don't want you to starve to death. It would be awkward to explain to your parents.'

'I doubt I'm in danger of starving anytime soon,' she said. She wasn't sure if he was making fun of her – compared to some of the girls at her school, she was a massive balloon that floated over the crowd at big parades – but it didn't seem that way. The idea of her parents made her stomach turn a little. She checked her phone. One o'clock. Her mom would be home any second, would discover Gemma was missing, and would send out an Amber Alert.

'Fine. But you're in danger of turning into a walking toothpick, like Chloe. Every time I see her, I feel like I have something in my teeth.'

She liked him a hundred times more for saying it, even if it wasn't true. She couldn't help it. Chloe looked like pretty girls were supposed to look, at least according to every fashion magazine and blog. And Gemma looked like the girl who'd *swallowed* the pretty girl.

She dug her hand in the bag and popped fries in her mouth. They were delicious. She didn't care that when she leaned forward her stomach rolled a little over her waistband. Pete wasn't even looking at her. He was busy scarfing his own burger. Gemma decided she liked the way he ate – with total attention, like the food was a complex math problem he had to solve.

'So you really didn't steal Chloe's underwear?' she asked after a moment.

''Course not,' he said, although since his mouth was full it came out *cough noff.* He made a big show of swallowing. 'Want to know my theory? My theory,' he said, without waiting for her to respond, 'is that Chloe DeWitt was and is hopelessly in love with me, and when I didn't steal her underwear, it drove her crazy. She had to pretend that I did.'

Gemma stared at him. There was a little bit of sauce at the corner of his mouth and she had the momentary urge to reach out and wipe it off. 'You're insane. Do you know that? You actually might be certifiable.'

He shook his head. His expression turned serious. 'Those girls are clones, Gemma. They lack brains.'

She turned toward the window so she would stop noticing things about him — how nice and long his hands were, with freckles sprinkled across the knuckles. His funny Adam's apple, which rioted up and down his throat when he spoke. Even if he was nice, he was still a cute boy, and cute boys did not go for girls like Gemma. She'd seen enough romantic comedies to know it.

'Clones have brains,' she said. 'You're thinking of zombies.'

'Zombie clones, then,' he said, and put the car in drive.

# SEVEN

THEY WERE NEARING JACKSONVILLE WHEN they heard about the explosion off Barrel Key, and the fire burning out of control on Spruce Island. Gemma had been searching the radio for something that wouldn't tempt Pete to sing along. It turned out when he wasn't talking, he was singing, usually off-key, and with some random jumble of words that had only a vague relationship to the *actual* lyrics. She was looking for gospel, bluegrass, hard-core rap, *anything*. The first hour of impromptu karaoke had been all right – she'd actually enjoyed his rendition of 'Man in the Mirror' and had nearly peed her pants when it turned out he knew every word to Britney Spears's '. . . Baby One More Time' – but after the second hour she longed for quiet, especially since Pete wouldn't stop harassing her about singing along.

When she hit a news station, she almost skipped right over it.

'– local officials confirmed the fire . . . at the Haven Institute for –'

'Come on, DJ, how about playing a song?' Pete spun away from the station just as Gemma froze, stunned. The radio skipped to a Jimmy Buffett song.

'No. Stop. Go back, please.' Gemma turned the radio back, past the crackle and hiss of silent frequencies, until she heard the newscaster's voice tune in again.

'. . . unconfirmed rumors . . . a deliberate attack . . .'

Pete was pretending to pout. 'Jimmy Buffett, Gemma. That's, like, Florida's national anthem. I think it's mandatory that we hear "Margaritaville" at least once a day. Otherwise we might get kicked out of the state.'

'I'm begging you. *Please.* This is important, okay?' She cranked the volume button, but the sound quality was awful. She had no idea where the station was broadcasting from, but it must have been closer to Barrel Key, and the voices kept patching in and out, interspersed with snippets of music from another station.

'Tom, is it true . . . actually took credit on Facebook?'

'. . . problem is . . . nobody talking . . .'

'Police say stay away until . . . situation under control . . .'

'Military presence . . .'

'Rumors of a protest at Barrel Key . . .'

But by then the interference was too great, and they were listening to some old-timey singer warbling about heartbreak. Gemma punched the radio off. She needed silence to think. There was a fire at Spruce Island – possibly an attack. But by whom? And what did it mean? Why would anyone attack a research institute? She thought of the man who'd grabbed her in the parking lot, with his coffee-stink breath and the wide frenzy of his eyes.

'Barrel Key,' Pete said slowly. For once, he wasn't smiling or twitching or trying to make her laugh. He was just frowning, holding tight to the steering wheel with both hands. 'That's where you're going, isn't it?'

'That's where you're going to take me,' Gemma said. And maybe it was the way she said it, or the way she looked, but he finally stayed quiet after that.

They got to Barrel Key just after six o'clock. Gemma had powered down her phone hours earlier, after sending a single text to her mom – *Gone to see April in Florida* – just so Kristina wouldn't be tempted to call out the police or the National Guard. Still, she knew her mom would be frantic. She had probably called Gemma's dad by now, too, and this gave Gemma her only satisfaction: he was thousands and thousands of miles away and couldn't punish her.

Barrel Key was one long chain of warehouses and boat

shops, big metal storehouses and bait-and-tackle shacks leaning over on their foundations. The sky, she noticed, was greenish, and only when she rolled her window down and the acrid smell of burning reached her did she realize that the wind had carried ash from Spruce Island.

'Wow,' Pete said as they passed a single motel, the *M* in its sign burned out, buzzing the word *vacancy* at them like a threat. 'Great vacation spot. Very, um, authentic.'

'It's more of a working vacation,' she said, because she knew he wouldn't drop it otherwise.

'What kind of work? You a world-class fly fisherman or something? Or trying to re-up on ammunition?' This as they were passing a lean-to advertising both *farm-fresh eggs* and major firearms. 'Do you want to tell me what you're really doing here?'

Gemma hesitated. 'I can't,' she said. It wasn't a lie. She didn't know exactly what she expected to find, only that the universe seemed to be pointing here, toward Haven. A battered sign showed the way to the marina. 'Turn right here.'

She kept the window down, straining for a glimpse of Spruce Island, but the buildings kept intruding and the ocean was only visible in brief flashes. Here, at least, the town was not nice, exactly, but nicer: another motel, this one with all its letters intact; diners and bars, stores with colorful lures displayed in the windows, a T-shirt shop and a restaurant with outdoor seating. In the distance she heard a sound she thought must be the roar of waves, but as they grew closer she made out human voices. A helicopter passed overhead, then another.

The road curved and they were prevented from going any farther by a series of sawhorses in the road and cops grimly gesturing them to turn around. Beyond the roadblock was the marina, and hundreds and hundreds of people gathered there, shouting and chanting and waving homemade signs. Beyond them, the spiky masts of small sailboats bobbing up and down in the water. A column of smoke was visible here, tufting up into the sky from somewhere up the coast and smearing the sun to a strange orange color.

A cop rapped on the driver's-side window, and Pete rolled it down. 'You're going to have to turn around,' the cop said. He was suited up in riot gear and carrying three guns that Gemma could see.

'That's where we're going,' Gemma said, gesturing to the angry crowd at the marina, and Pete gave her a look like, *We are?*

'Turn around,' the cop said. 'Nothing to see here.'

'Except for the huge fireball and all the people going nutty,' Pete said. Gemma elbowed him as the cop leaned down to stare at them through the window. 'But otherwise you're right, nothing to see. Nothing at all.' A second cop was moving toward them, and Pete quickly put the car in reverse. 'Have a nice day!' he shouted, even as he was backing haphazardly up the street. The two cops stood there, staring after them, until they'd turned around in the parking lot of a hardware store and started back in the direction they'd come.

'Well, *that* was a lovely day trip,' Pete said as they left the marina behind. 'Where to now? Any natural disasters you want to visit? Prison camps? Political riots?'

Gemma spotted a vacant parking lot behind a long line of low-ceilinged storage units. 'Pull over here,' she said.

Pete turned to stare at her. 'Are you serious?'

'Please. Just do it.' It felt good to give orders, to have a plan, to be out on her own, to do what she wanted without having to beg for permission. Something leapt to life in her chest, a force beyond the guilt and the fear. It was like she'd been living in a cartoon, in two dimensions, her whole life, and had just fought free of the page.

He did, barely making the turn, and rolled to a stop. 'Most people think of spring break, they think bikinis, virgin piña coladas, spray tans . . .'

'Not me,' Gemma said, trying to make a joke of it. 'I'm allergic to coconut. And I don't even *own* a bikini.'

'Why not?' His eyes were very clear when he turned to look at her. 'You'd look great in a bikini.'

Once again, she couldn't tell whether he was making

fun of her. There was an awkward second when Gemma was acutely aware that she was imagining Pete imagining *her* in a bikini, fat rolls and thighs that rubbed together and everything. She wanted to die of embarrassment. Her cheeks felt like someone had put a torch to them. She could hardly stand to look at him, but she had to know whether he was smirking.

He wasn't. He was fiddling nervously with the radio, even though he'd shut off the car ignition. It occurred to Gemma that he was nervous – actually nervous. Because of her.

*Germ* Ives. The Frankenstein monster.

'I'll be fine,' she said, and opened the car door. She didn't know where all the tension had come from, but she was desperate to escape it. Her whole body was torch-hot now. Immediately, the faint scent of burning reached her, and beneath it, the smell of swampland – sunbaked mud and belly-up fish and microorganisms wiggling deep in the earth. 'Thanks for the ride. Really.'

'You *are* serious,' he said, as though he couldn't believe it. He raised his hands. 'All right. Whatever gets your goat.'

'*Whatever gets your goat?*' She shook her head, amazed.

'Yeah. You know. Whatever wets your whistle, gets your rocks off, brings you to your happy place –'

'Pete?' she said. But she couldn't help but smile.

'Know when to stop. Seriously.'

She got out of the car, half expecting him to call her back. But he popped the trunk when she rapped on it and she slung her backpack over her shoulder, still with that weird sense of guilt and fear arm-wrestling with excitement in her stomach. Pete rolled down the window and called out to her before she could walk away.

'You'll call me, right? If you need anything?'

'Is this your fancy way of getting my number?' Gemma asked. Immediately she wanted to chew her own lips off. She sounded like such a dork. And she hated herself for caring, too. He'd given her a ride and that was it. It wasn't like they'd been on a date.

'Technically,' he said, 'it's my fancy way of making you *ask* for my number.' He smiled at her all crookedly, with his hair standing up as if it was happy, too. She took his number down and he took hers. 'Promise you'll call, all right? So I know you didn't end up, you know, eaten by a crocodile or something?'

She promised she would, although she knew she wouldn't – besides, he was just being polite. She stood there and waved good-bye, feeling a quick squeeze of regret as Pete bumped off onto the road in his ridiculous van. If she was honest, she had to admit she hadn't *hated* hanging out with him. He was annoying, obviously. She didn't like the way that he looked at her sometimes, as if his eyes were lasers boring straight into her brain. But he was funny, and he was company, and he was, okay, maybe-kind-of cute. She'd never even been alone with a boy before today.

Now she was definitely alone.

She turned back toward the marina. As soon as she began walking, she regretted telling Pete to drop her off so far away. She couldn't approach the marina head on. She had no desire for face time with RoboCop and his buddy. But she figured if she could find a different route onto the beach, she could make her way back along the water to the place where everyone had gathered. Then, she hoped, she'd be able to figure out what had happened at Haven – what Haven *was*, even.

When she could hear the noise of the protest, she turned left and cut through a rutted, salt-worn alley between two boat shops, and then right on a street parallel to the one that led to the marina. Beach grass grew between cracks of the asphalt and a fine layer of sand coated the sidewalks. The houses here were interspersed with smoke shops and dingy bodegas, each of them painted a different pastel but also dusty and dim-looking, like old photographs leached of their luster. After another minute, the buildings fell back and she saw the water flashing behind saw grass the color of spun caramel. A chain-link fence blocked passage down to the beach, and beyond it she saw rusted kayaks piled in the grass and a scattering of broken beer bottles and cigarettes. She looked behind her: no movement in any of the houses, no signs of life at all except for a skinny cat slinking out from underneath an old Toyota Corolla. Several more helicopters motored by overhead.

She removed her backpack and heaved it over the fence, and then, checking once again to make sure no one was looking, interlaced her fingers in the chain-link and began to climb. The fence swayed dangerously and she had a momentary vision of toppling backward and pulling the whole fence with her. She maneuvered clumsily over the top of the fence and then dropped to the sand, breathing hard now and sweating under the strange smoky sun. She picked up her backpack, realizing as she did that she could now see Spruce Island in the distance – or at least, what she thought must be Spruce Island. About a mile up the coast she could make out a range of heavy dark growth above the horizon. The rest of the island, and whatever Haven was or had been, was blurred by a scrim of smoke and heat.

She picked her way along this untended portion of beach back toward the marina, watching her feet so she didn't trip on any of the junk embedded in the sand. She came to another chain-link fence, this one running down into the water, but luckily found a gate unlatched and didn't have to climb again. Then she was in front of a battered gray warehouse. She'd seen it at an angle from Pete's car and knew that it extended like a long arm to brace one side of the marina.

And now the swell of voices reached her over the wind. She had to slosh down into the mud to get around the old warehouse, and every time she stepped, a few inches of filthy water swirled up around her shoes. On the far side of the warehouse was the parking lot the police had blocked off, and the crowd had assembled there, some people carrying signs and chanting in unison, some camped out on the asphalt with picnic blankets and binoculars, like they were at a summer concert. A few kids Gemma's age or slightly older were grouped along the edge of a neighboring roof, legs dangling like icicles from the eaves, watching the action. Gemma counted fifty people and at least a dozen cops. What was going on at Haven that it would be so worth protecting? Or destroying?

She slipped unnoticed into the crowd.

She passed a man wearing a plastic Viking helmet that had been outfitted with different antennae and metal coils. He kept pacing in circles, gesturing to an invisible audience and muttering, and when he caught Gemma looking, he whirled on her and continued his monologue even more loudly '– and why we couldn't drink any of the water when we were stationed in Nasiriyah, fear of poison, of course some must have gone in the food supply and that's why the doctor says holes in my brain –'

She turned quickly away. Several people wore gas masks that made them look like the bad guys in a horror film, or like enormous insects, which made it even weirder that they were standing around in jeans and beat-up Top-Siders, gazing out over the water. The protesters, she saw, were calling for Haven's shuttering. *Our Land, Our Health, Our Right,* read one sign, and another said, *Keep Your Chemicals Out of My Backyard.* But among them were signs with other, stranger messages: signs that referenced Roswell and Big Brother and zombies, and several posters screaming about the dangers of hell. One girl who couldn't have been older than twelve was holding a colorful handmade sign with bubbly letters: *And Cast Ye the Unprofitable Servant into Outer Darkness.*

Gemma picked out a sunburned middle-aged couple who looked normal enough and fought her way over to them. The man wore leather sandals and a baseball hat with the logo of a hunting lodge on it. The woman was wearing a fanny pack. Both of them were staring out toward the billowing clouds of smoke in the distance, which made it look as if a volcano had erupted mid-ocean.

'What's going on?' Gemma asked them. It was funny how disasters made friends of everyone. 'Is anyone saying how the fire started?'

The man shook his head. 'Nothing official. Heard

maybe a gas line blew up. Of course the island's loaded with chemicals, would have caught fast −'

His wife snorted. 'It was no gas line,' she said. 'We've talked to a dozen locals say they heard at least two explosions, one right after another.'

'Explosions,' Gemma repeated, shifting the backpack strap on her shoulder. Sweat had gathered under the collar of her shirt. 'Like a bomb or something?'

The woman gave Gemma a pitying look. 'You're not from around here, are you? People have been calling for the institute or whatever it is to be shut down for years now. I wouldn't be surprised if someone decided to take a shortcut. Of course the rumors . . .' She spread her hands.

'What kind of rumors?' Gemma pressed, although she remembered from the Haven Files a long list of all the different things supposedly manufactured at Haven − everything from incredibly contagious diseases to human organs.

'Some people think they got aliens out there on that island,' the husband said. Now Gemma understood the reference to Roswell, where an alien spaceship had supposedly crashed and then been concealed by the military. 'Well, I tell you, we come up every year from Orlando to do a little paddling and bird-watching in the reserve. Great birds up here − white ibis, knots, and dowitchers on the old oyster bars. You interested in birds?' Gemma arranged her face into what she hoped was a polite expression and nodded. He harrumphed as if he didn't believe it and went on, 'I've got a pair of binoculars can spot a pine grosbeak at a distance of eight hundred yards, and I've done a little sighting of the island and never seen any glowing green men.' He kept his eyes on the fire in the distance. 'But I'll tell you they have guards in mounted towers, barbed-wire fences sixteen feet high. They'll shoot you if you get too close and won't blink about it. They say they're doing medical research out there, stuff for our boys overseas, but I don't buy it. They're hiding something, that's for sure.'

Another chopper went by overhead, and Gem felt the staccato of its giant rotor all the way in her chest. It seemed obvious that no one knew what was happening or had happened out in Haven, but still she fought through the crowd, searching for an official, for someone in charge. Forcing her way through the knot of protesters, she saw a policeman arguing with a dark-haired boy with the kind of symmetrical good looks that Gemma associated with movies about superheroes. The cop was holding a professional-looking camera and appeared to be deleting pictures.

'. . . no right to confiscate it,' the boy was saying, as Gemma approached. 'That's private property.'

'What did I say about taking pictures?' the cop said,

angling away and blocking the boy with a shoulder when he tried to reach for his camera. 'This isn't the goddamn Grand Canyon. We've got an emergency on our hands. Show some respect.'

Gemma couldn't help but feel sorry for the boy. He looked furious. He couldn't have been much older than she was, and the camera looked expensive. 'I'm not a tourist,' he said. 'And I can take pictures if I want to. This is America.'

'This is a crime scene, at least until we say otherwise,' the cop said.

The boy clenched his fists. Gemma found herself momentarily frozen, watching him. For a second his eyes ticked to hers, but they swept away just as quickly. She wasn't offended. She was used to being invisible to other people, preferred it, even.

'All right.' The cop had finished with the camera. He popped open the back of the camera, removed the battery, and then returned the now-useless camera to Jake. 'Now for your phone, please.'

'You can't be serious.' The boy had gone completely white. Gemma was getting angry on his behalf. Why wouldn't he have the right to take pictures if he wanted to?

The cop was obviously losing patience. He raised a finger and jabbed it right in the boy's face. 'Now look here, son —'

'My name is Jake,' the boy said smoothly. 'Jake Witz.'

'All right, Jake Witz. You want to make trouble, you just keep on yapping. But I'll bring you down to the station –'

'For what? Having an iPhone?'

'That mouth is gonna get you into trouble. . . .'

Gemma was too stunned to move. Jake Witz was the name of the guy who ran the Haven Files website. It had to be a coincidence – he bore no resemblance to the guy in the profile picture on the site. This guy looked like he could be a Clark Kent body double, just without the glasses.

And yet . . . When she looked closer, she thought she saw certain similarities. The line of the boy's jaw, which in the older man had been blurred. The same slightly-too-large nose, which on the boy looked strong and perfect and on the older man had just looked comical. Relatives, then? She couldn't be sure.

Finally the boy had no choice but to pass over his phone. The cop made Jake unlock the screen, and then sorted through the pictures, deleting the ones he deemed inappropriate. Jake stood there, his face hard with anger, which somehow made him even *more* attractive.

Finally the cop returned the phone and gave Jake a big thump on the back, as if they were best friends at a baseball game. 'Good man,' he said. 'Now don't make me ask you again, all right? Clear on out of here. Nothing to see.'

Almost immediately, the cop swaggered away, pushing roughly past Gemma without sparing her a second glance, this time to yell at two teenage girls who were trying to record a video with their phones. Jake aimed a kick at a crushed Coca-Cola can, which skittered across the sand and gravel and landed in a patch of grass. Either he hadn't noticed Gemma or he was pretending not to have.

So she cleared her throat. 'Jake? Jake Witz?'

He looked up finally and her heart stuttered. His eyes were large and dark and mournful, and reminded her of the way Rufus looked when no one was paying him any attention.

'Yeah?' he said. He sounded tired. He looked tired, too, and she wondered how long he'd been out here, watching.

'My name's Gemma Ives,' she said. She realized she hadn't exactly planned what she was going to say. She still didn't know what connection this Jake Witz had to the guy who ran the Haven Files, or whether there *was* a connection. If he recognized her last name, he gave no indication of it. 'I know you. Well, I know of you. You're from the Haven Files, right?'

He frowned. 'The website was my dad's thing,' he

said. 'I have nothing to do with it.' He started to turn away.

'You must have *something* to do with it,' Gemma said. The words leapt out of her mouth before she could stop them. Slowly he turned back to face her.

'What's that supposed to mean?'

Gemma licked her lips. 'You're here, aren't you?' she said. 'We're about as close as we can get to Haven. You're taking pictures. You must be interested, at least a little.'

He didn't agree. But he didn't deny it, either. He just stood there, watching her. Gemma couldn't tell whether he found her amusing or irritating. His face was too perfect. It was unreadable. Just being around him made her feel like she was fumbling her way through a restaurant that was far too fancy for her. She found if she avoided looking directly in his eyes, and instead focused her attention on his nose or eyebrows or cheekbones, she could at least think.

'Look,' she said. 'I came all the way from North Carolina. My dad was involved with Haven somehow, or at least people *think* he was involved. He's not scared of anything, but he's scared of that. I want to know why. I have to know what they do at Haven. I have to know why it matters to him.' *And to me,* she added silently.

For a long time, Jake said nothing. Then, just for a second, a smile went fast across his face. 'Not by a long shot,' he said, so quietly that Gemma wasn't sure he meant for her to hear. He started to turn around again, and Gemma's heart sank.

'What did you say?' She was sure, now, that fate had led her here, to Jake Witz. Sure that no matter what he claimed, he knew the truth about Haven.

'You said we were as close as we could get to Haven. But we're not. Not even close.' He inclined his head and Gemma recognized the gesture for what it was: an invitation. He wanted her to follow him. This time, his smile was real, and long, and nearly blinded her. 'Come on, Gemma Ives. I've been in the sun all day. I could do with a waffle.'

Jake explained that there were two ways out to Haven. One was to take a launch from Barrel Key and circle around to the far side of the island, where the coast dissolved into open ocean, staying clear of the marshes. This was the way the passenger boats ferried employees back and forth, and the way that freight was moved. No boat of any size could navigate the marshes.

But there was another way: the Wahlee River, which passed the tiny fishing village of Wahlee and fanned out into the marshes – miles of winding, narrow channels and half-submerged islands that reached nearly all the way to Haven's northern coast.

'How do you know all this?' Gemma asked. They'd found a diner tucked off the main drag, empty except for a mom and her toddler and two older men in hunting vests huddled over coffee, with faces so chewed up by wind and weather it looked like their skin was in the process of dissolving. Although from here the ocean was invisible, there was still a rubber-stink smell in the air, and they could hear the occasional threshing of helicopters overhead.

Jake lined up four containers of half-and-half and emptied them one by one into his coffee. 'I've lived in Little Waller my whole life,' he said. 'That's forty miles from here. My dad was big into fishing, camping, that kind of thing. We used to camp on the Wahlee. Spruce Island used to be owned by some timber company but Haven bought them out to build the institute. I remember they were still doing construction on some of the buildings when I was a kid.' He shrugged. 'Maybe that's when his obsession started. I never got the chance to ask.'

Gemma swallowed. 'Is he . . . ?'

'Dead,' Jake said matter-of-factly, without looking at her. He stirred his coffee with a spoon but didn't drink. 'Died four years ago, when I was fourteen. Drowned in the marshes. That's what they said, anyway.'

Gemma felt suddenly cold. 'What do you mean?'

Jake just shook his head. He leaned forward on his

elbows, staring out the window, and was quiet for a bit. A small TV mounted above the coffeepot was tuned to the news and kept scanning across the marina they'd just left behind. The waitress, a woman with hair shellacked into a bun, was parked in front of the TV with her arms crossed.

'I never really understood my dad,' Jake said. His voice was rough, as if it were sliding over gravel. 'He wasn't like the other dads. He worked at one of the plants cleaning out fish guts, but he carried a business card everywhere like he was the president of the United States or something, never left the house without a blazer, no matter what else he was wearing, Bermuda shorts or a bathing suit. He was always talking about his *theories*. He talked so goddamn much. He used to joke that's why my mom left, because she couldn't stand the talk. But I don't know. He might've been right. As a kid I just wanted him to shut up sometimes, you know?' He leaned back, meeting Gemma's eyes again, and she was startled by their darkness, their intensity. She couldn't help thinking that Jake and Pete were complete opposites: Pete walked like he was jumping, Jake as if the gravity were double for him what it was for anyone else. Pete was all lightness, Jake all weight. 'I was ashamed of him, you know? Even as a kid, I was ashamed. Does that make me a bad person?'

'No,' Gemma whispered.

He smiled as if he didn't believe her. He was neatening his empty plate, lining up his silverware with the table, his cup and saucer with the plate. He was the neatest eater Gemma had ever seen. She was embarrassed to see a ketchup blob and some crumbs by her elbow, and quickly wiped them up when he wasn't looking.

'My dad liked to say he missed his calling as a journalist. He always saw cover-ups, conspiracies, that kind of thing. JFK was killed because he was about to do a public memorandum on sentient life on other planets. Chicken pox was actually a biological agent released from a government lab. But Haven. Haven was his white whale.' Jake pressed his hands flat against the table, hard, as if he could squeeze the memory of his father out through his palms. Even his *fingers* were perfect. 'He used to take me with him on fishing trips out on the marshes. Or at least, I *thought* they were fishing trips, at first.'

'Reconnaissance,' Gemma said.

Jake nodded. 'Being on the marshes is like being inside a maze. Red maple and cordgrass, needle rush, palmetto – it grows ten, twelve feet high and swallows up the horizon. My dad had friends who'd gotten lost for hours, even days out there, floating around trying to lick water from plant leaves and eating grubs for dinner and there they were, not a half mile from camp. Once we got really close, within shouting distance of the island. Well, all of a sudden there must have been eight, ten guards with guns, shouting for us to turn around and head back. My dad was furious. I was just a kid, you know. They acted like they were about to blow our heads off. They probably would have. They've fired on people before, civilians. I know a fisherman from town, says he almost got a hand blown off. Says he thinks it must have been a sniper to get him from that distance. Of course they're all from the military.' He shook his head, smiling faintly. 'In all the years I've lived down here, I know of only one person who made it onto the island – some kid snuck under a bad bit of fence in the middle of the night. Got chucked out just as quickly.'

Gemma was having trouble following everything that Jake was saying, but she understood the main points: crazy-tight security, no one allowed to talk. 'What about the people who work out there?' she asked. 'The guards and the staff? *Someone* must be going on and off the island.'

Jake nodded. 'Freight goes in and out, sure, and trash gets collected on Sundays. But no one goes past the gate. The staff goes out on launches from town. Some of them live there and come back to the mainland on leave. Some of them commute. But they won't talk. They won't say a word about what goes on there. Like they're all scared.'

He took a breath. 'Everyone except for Nurse M.'

'Nurse M?' Gemma repeated. 'Who's Nurse M?'

'I wish I knew.' This time, Jake's smile was crooked, as if he was too tired to make it line up. 'Before he died, my dad said he was working some big angle. He said he was going to blow the lid off the whole operation. That's how he talked, you know. Like we were all cast members of some Hollywood spy movie.' A look of pain seized him momentarily. 'He told me he'd found a woman, Nurse M, who'd agreed to talk to him. She wanted everyone to know the truth. But the day before they were supposed to meet up, she died. Killed herself, allegedly.' He straightened his fork and knife again, avoiding Gemma's eyes.

Although it was warm in the diner, Gemma felt as if a cold tongue had just licked the back of her neck. 'But you don't believe that,' she said slowly, watching him. He shrugged. 'You think she was . . . murdered? So she wouldn't be able to talk?'

Now he picked at the surface of the table with a thumbnail. 'I don't know. But it looks strange, doesn't it?' He shook his head. 'My dad left notes. Tons and tons of notes about Haven, some of them nonsensical, some of them just irrelevant. I never found her real name. He was trying to protect her, I think. But he failed.'

Gemma felt suddenly nauseous. Her father was wrapped up in this. Her family was wrapped up in it. 'You said they told you your father drowned. You don't believe it.' She was afraid to ask. But she had to know.

He looked down at his lap. 'After that time we almost got shot, my dad stopped taking me with him when he went out on the marshes. He was scared. But he was getting closer, too. I know that now. He died only two months after Nurse M was found hanging. That's no coincidence.' A muscle in his jaw twitched. 'I still remember the smell of that morning, like this kind of aftershave one of the cops was wearing. Isn't that crazy? I can't remember his face, but I remember his goddamn aftershave.' He laughed softly. She had the urge to reach out and take his hand, but of course, she didn't. 'I was fourteen. They told me he'd been fishing when a storm blew in. Said he must have flipped his kayak, got turned around.'

'And what do you think?' Gemma said.

He looked up. His eyes were like twin holes. There was so much pain at the bottom of them, Gemma wanted to look away, but couldn't. 'My dad was a lot of things,' he said softly. 'But he wasn't an idiot. He could navigate those marshes blindfolded. He was happier on the water than anywhere else. He said it was the only place he belonged, you know?' He looked away again. Gemma wondered what it would be like to lose a parent so young, and found she couldn't imagine it. Would she be unhappy if her father died? She had always fantasized about simply deleting him from her life, pressing backspace and watching him vanish. But the truth, of course, was more complicated than that.

'What do you think really happened?' she asked.

He sighed. 'I think he made it,' he said. 'I think he got onto the island. And then I think he was caught. They would have made it look like an accident.'

Gemma felt as if there were a spider caught in her throat, trying to claw its way up her windpipe. She didn't want to believe any of it.

But she did.

'Do you know what they do at Haven?' Gemma asked. It was the question she'd come to Florida to answer – the only question that mattered.

'No,' Jake answered bluntly, and Gemma's heart fell. 'But I have some idea.'

She waited, almost afraid to breathe. Jake looked around the diner as though trying to judge whether they were safe. No one was paying them any attention. Still, he called out to the waitress. 'Excuse me? Would you mind turning up the volume?' he said. She barely glanced at him before punching up the volume on the remote.

A bug-eyed woman behind a news desk was staring earnestly into the camera, and for a moment Gemma latched on to her voice. '. . . Dr. Mark Saperstein, who is listed as the current director of the Haven Institute, cannot be reached for comment. It is unknown whether he too was on the island when the explosion . . .'

Jake leaned forward and cleared his throat. 'Human experimentation.'

'What?' Gemma looked away from the TV, which was again showing images of the coastline, and the sun setting behind a veil of smoke.

Jake shoved his hand through his hair. 'Human experimentation. I know it sounds crazy,' he added, before Gemma could say it. 'And I'm not talking about your usual drug trials, either. I'm talking illegal experimentation. Weapons development. Chemical trials. That's why all the security, and why they're so far out of the way. No oversight.'

Gemma frowned. Every medication or treatment that went to market had to go through human clinical trials. Gemma's dad was always railing against the medical ethics board's shortsightedness and how difficult it was to drum up volunteers for certain treatments. He was convinced that thousands of people died every year because the drugs that could have saved them were still being reviewed for safety by the FDA or hadn't been approved yet for human trial. Could Haven be a place designed so researchers could skirt the normal rules, and do their work with no oversight? She could understand, if so, why her father might have refused to pour money into Haven, and might have left Fine & Ives before his name could be associated with the deal. There had never been a bigger fan of rule following than Geoffrey Ives.

Still, the whole thing was pretty far-fetched. And it wouldn't explain why Gemma's father was so afraid. If he really had refused to participate, if he'd left his own company just to avoid the association with Haven, he would be praised as a hero.

'Where do they get the volunteers?' she asked. Her coffee was cold by now, but it was comforting to hold the mug between her palms.

Jake bit his lip, looking at her sideways. 'That's the point,' he says. 'I don't think they're volunteers.'

Gemma stared at him. 'What do you mean?'

'They're not *getting* volunteers – not for these experiments. They're forcing people to participate.'

'But . . . how?' Gemma asked. The french toast she'd eaten seemed to be sticking in her throat. 'They can't just – I don't know – kidnap people.'

'Why not?' Jake leaned forward. 'Look, Gemma. This was my dad's work. This was his life. However nuts it sounds, I think he was onto something. Fine and Ives has military contracts, money coming directly from the top. *Half* of Fine and Ives's budget comes from military contracts. This is the government we're taking about.'

Gemma thought of her father and his old company,

and her stomach squirmed. She remembered Christmas parties as a kid at the Carolina Inn, the ceiling draped in tinsel and plastic snowflakes, and everyone standing to applaud her father as he entered, clutching Gemma's hand. She remembered visiting the White House with her dad on a trip to DC, and how he shook the president's hand, and Gemma and her mother got to go downstairs to play ninepins in the White House bowling alley. And men suited up in crisp uniforms pinned with shiny medals going in and out of her father's office, smiling at her, hefting her into the air, tossing and catching her with big muscled arms.

Jake leaned forward, lowering his voice. 'You've heard of Dr. Saperstein?' Gemma nodded. She remembered reading that Dr. Saperstein had taken control of Haven after Richard Haven had died in a car accident – the very same year she was born. The coincidence now seemed ominous. 'About fifteen years ago, Saperstein weaseled his way onto the board of a nonprofit called the Home Foundation up in Philadelphia. It still exists today,' he added when Gemma shook her head to show she hadn't heard of it. 'He spent a few years growing its operations, expanding the volunteer forces, crowing about it in the media. Anyway, my dad dug up all the details. The Home Foundation places kids in foster care. These are the worst cases, children who've bounced around for years, or got dumped in front of the fire station or the hospital. It was the perfect setup. Kids get shuffled and reshuffled, moved around, drop out of the system, run away, disappear. Nobody's going to look too hard for them, right?'

Gemma felt now as if her thoughts were all gummed up and sticky. Maple Syrup Brain. 'I don't get it,' she said. 'What are you saying? You can't mean −' She took a deep breath. 'They're not doing experiments on kids?'

'They're *only* doing experiments on kids,' Jake said gently − almost apologetically, Gemma thought. 'I think Saperstein stole them. He stole them and brought them to Haven. That's why all the security. It's not just to keep us out, you know. Not by a long shot. It's to keep them in.'

Gemma felt dizzy, even though she hadn't moved. It was too terrible. She didn't want to believe it. She wouldn't believe it. 'There's no proof,' she said. Her voice sounded tinny and far away, as if she was hearing it through a pipe.

Jake turned to look out the window. The smoke was still smudging the horizon, turning the setting sun to a smoldering orange. He said something so quietly Gemma nearly missed it.

Nearly.

Suddenly her heart was beating so hard, it felt as if it might burst through her chest.

'What?' she said. 'What did you just say?'

He sighed. This time when he looked at her, she was afraid.

'I saw them,' he repeated.

'How?' Gemma felt like she was choking.

'Remember that boy I told you about, the one who made it onto Haven through the fence?' Jake half smiled. 'I was the boy.'

# EIGHT

THE TWO BASS MOTEL WAS just outside of town – a long, low, shingle-sided building with only a single car in the parking lot. When Gemma requested a room, the ancient owner knocked over her tea in surprise, as if she'd never before heard the words. But the room was clean, although slightly musty-smelling, and decorated, predictably, with lots of fish: an itchy coverlet woven with images of leaping salmon, a framed picture of fly-fishing hooks above the TV, a plastic bass mounted on the wall in the bathroom. Gemma hoped it wasn't the singing kind.

They had agreed that Jake would come back for her at eleven o'clock, and Gemma wasn't sure what was making her so nervous – the idea of trying to sneak into Haven, as Jake had done only once before, or the idea of being alone with him in the dark.

Alone with those perfect hands and eyes and lashes and

fingernail beds. She'd never even *noticed* fingernail beds before. But she'd noticed his.

She powered on her phone. There was a sudden frenzied beeping as a dozen texts and voice mails loaded, and she was surprised to see among all the messages from her mom that Pete had already texted her.

*You didn't get eaten by an alligator, did you?*

For a quick second, she actually felt guilty, as if she was cheating on Jake. Then, of course, she felt like an idiot. A delusional idiot.

She wrote back: *I'd like to see one try.*

Then she dialed April's number.

April picked up on the first ring and was talking before Gemma could even say hello.

'Thank God, finally, I've been calling you for, like, five hours. I thought you said your parents *caved*, but your mom is freaking out, she said you basically *ran away*, I mean, seriously, I'm talking about National Guard, Armageddon-level freak-out, if screaming were a superpower, she'd seriously be eligible for her own franchise –'

'Did you tell her I was with you?' Gemma asked quickly. The idea of her mother screaming – or even raising her voice – was both difficult to imagine and also terrifying. Her dad was the screamer. Her mom was the apologizer, the mediator, the smoother-over. The nothing-a-glass-of-wine-and-a-Klonopin-can't-fix kind of person.

April snorted. 'Do you think I'm a complete amoeba? Of course I did. Except I started running out of reasons you wouldn't come to the phone. First I said you were napping, then that you'd gone out for a swim, then that you were in town getting coffee, and then I had to stop picking up the phone. I'm talking serious harassment here, she's probably called, like, twenty times —'

'I'll call her, okay? I'll call her right now,' Gemma said, and April let out a big *whoosh* of air.

'Please,' she said. 'Before your mom calls in a SWAT team. My grandpa will kill me if they trample his geraniums.' And then, in a different voice: 'Where *are* you? Are you okay? How did you even get down here?'

'I'm in Barrel Key, not far away,' Gemma said, avoiding April's last question, tracing one of the fish patterned on her coverlet with a finger. All the fish were identical, and all of them had the same anatomical error, an extra fin on the back that gave them a vaguely prehistoric look.

'But what are you doing *there*? I thought you were coming to stay with me.'

'I am. Tomorrow. And then I'll tell you everything. I *promise*,' Gemma said, before April could protest. She'd already lied so much in the past twenty-four hours. She couldn't stand lying to April, too. But what could she say to explain? *Oh, no big deal, someone threw a Frankenstein mask through our window and then a random psycho tried to*

GEMMA

**102**

LYRA

*nab me from a gas station and I think it's because my dad's old company is kidnapping children and testing chemicals on them and he might have known about it all this time.* 'Just trust me, okay?'

April sighed. 'Swear you're not holed up in some seedy motel meeting a stranger named Danger66 who claims to be a French exchange student looking for an English tutor.'

Gemma looked around the room, and decided it definitely counted as a seedy motel. 'I promise I'm not meeting a stranger named Danger66,' she said. 'I promise I'm not meeting *any* stranger.' Jake Witz blinked momentarily in her mind. But he didn't count. She'd sought him out, not the other way around. Besides, she couldn't believe that someone who looked like Jake Witz could be dangerous. She'd been fed a steady diet of Disney growing up. The evil ones were always ugly. By the same logic, she knew that she was destined to be the charming dumpy sidekick for life: only skinny girls got to be leads.

Her next phone call went far less smoothly. April was right. Her mom was in full-on panic mode. Gemma had never heard her mother so upset, except for one time when she was a little kid and decided to smash up her mom's favorite necklace with a hammer to see whether diamonds were really the hardest substance on earth.

'I don't believe you. I really don't believe you. I would

never have expected it, never in a million years – after we specifically told you –'

'Mom, calm down.' Gemma was annoyed not by the injustice of her parents' rules but by the fact that her mom had automatically assumed she would always obey. Just like she'd obeyed as a kid, shivering in those hospital beds, swallowing pills when she was told to swallow them, waking up with new scars, new evidence of damage. 'It's not a big deal, okay?'

'Not a big deal? Not a big deal?' Kristina seemed to be gasping the words. 'How can you even say that? Do you know how worried I've been? How worried your *father's* been?'

'Yeah. I'm sure he's been crying into his PowerPoint.' The words were out of Gemma's mouth as soon as she thought them.

Kristina drew in a sharp breath. Then she said, in a quiet voice, 'For your information, your father is on his way back from Shanghai right now. As soon as he lands, we're getting on a plane and coming straight down to get you –'

'Mom, no.' Gemma was surprised that in an instant, all her anger was gone, and instead she was suddenly on the verge of tears. She took a deep breath. 'Please,' she said, because she knew that fighting or yelling wouldn't help. 'I'm not in trouble. I'm safe. I'm with April.' She no longer felt guilty about lying. If Jake was right about what they were doing at Haven, her father must have known about it, and had spent his whole life lying – her mother, too. It was like she'd heard him say: he'd done nothing. 'Please let me have this, just this once. Let me be normal.'

Kristina sighed, and Gemma knew she'd said the right thing. She imagined her mother cradling the phone against one shoulder, unscrewing the cap of one of her pill bottles and shaking one into her palm, starting to calm down.

'I'll talk to your dad,' she said. 'But you know how he is. He's furious. You lied to us, Gemma.'

*How many times have you lied to me?* Gemma nearly said. But she swallowed the words back. She said instead, 'You didn't give me much choice.'

To her surprise, her mother laughed. But it was the saddest laugh ever, like she really wanted to cry. 'We're just trying to keep you safe, Gem,' she said. 'That's all we ever wanted.'

'I'm safe,' she said. 'I'm fine.'

When Kristina spoke again, her voice was softer. Probably just the *thought* of a pill working its way through her bloodstream had calmed her. 'I expect you to call me first thing in the morning.'

'I will,' Gem said. 'Just tell Dad not to worry.'

Kristina hesitated. 'I'll see what I can do.'

Gemma hung up. She was briefly euphoric, almost dizzy, but the feeling was short-lived. She'd gotten her mom only temporarily off her back. If her dad insisted on driving straight to April's house . . . if he discovered she wasn't there . . .

But if everything went as planned, she could make it to April's by morning, when her dad was still thirty thousand feet over the Atlantic. If everything went as planned, she might have all the answers she needed tonight.

And then what? What did it matter, really?

She wasn't sure. But she sensed − no, she *knew* − that there was in Haven a reason for her dad's constant, simmering anger; for the pills her mom measured out day by day; for the vast silence that filled her house and the way she caught her parents looking at her sometimes, as if she were a stranger.

She had to know why.

Her phone pinged. She assumed it would be her mom, calling back, but saw she had a new message from Pete: a GIF of a cartoon cowboy wrangling an alligator.

She tried watching TV but couldn't get anything but a blinking error message. She was nervous about what they were about to attempt, which was more dangerous than anything she'd ever even considered − she'd once nearly crapped herself cutting gym class to hang out with April like badasses behind the tennis courts. She wished she were the kind of girl who, when nervous, lost her appetite. Instead she made four trips to the vending machine, which contained only a few warm sodas, some Kit Kats, cardboard-tasting chips, and a bag of ancient Sour Patch Kids, shriveled and dry as discarded husks of molted cicadas.

She searched for more news about what had happened at Haven, refreshing the few local news sites that were covering it and toggling back and forth between individual blogs and conspiracy sites. The explosion had renewed public interest in Haven. She found a couple of news sites that referenced the controversy from several years ago, in which Haven was listed as one of the research institutes that had illegally purchased human tissue for research, including embryonic and stem cells. She knew embryonic cells were used for medical research. It fit Jake's theory. Fine & Ives had even released a statement, a bland PR document about a sudden fire at one of their research institutes. Every article had attracted dozens of comments, many of them nonsensical or filled with curses and hysterical references to escaped biological agents.

Around nine she saw references on several sites to a terrorist attack, by an individual who supposedly believed she was acting on God's commandment and had somehow managed to infiltrate the island. But there was frustratingly little information about the attack, and after only twenty minutes, many of the individual story links had been disabled or taken down. She was halfway through an article about the possibility that the person responsible had managed to stow away on the ferry that collected the waste from Haven twice a week when the whole page just blinked and then went dark, as if someone had pulled a curtain over her screen. She reloaded the page several times but kept getting the same 404 error.

'What the hell?' She jabbed her screen with a finger, trying to figure out how a webpage could just disappear while she was looking at it. There was a knock at the door and she jumped. She'd lost track of time completely. It was eleven o'clock already.

Jake had changed into a black T-shirt, dark jeans, and black Vans. When Gemma opened the door, she thought he looked like the lead singer in some indie band April might have been obsessed with. She wished temporarily she'd done something with her hair – more delusion. As if a great hairstyle would distract him from the thirty extra pounds she was packing.

He came into the room without saying hello and sat down on the bed.

'Did you hear?' he said. When he shoved a hand through his hair, it resettled right away. Soft, then. Of course. 'The cops traced the explosion.'

She closed the door and leaned against it. It occurred to her that this was exactly what she'd sworn to April she wouldn't do – meet a stranger in a seedy motel room. Maybe she'd sit down next to him and he'd try and touch her thigh or force his tongue down her throat. Then again, she wouldn't mind. If anyone was in danger of getting sexually harassed, it was probably him.

Jake pulled out a laptop from his backpack. 'This came into my in-box an hour ago.' He pivoted his computer screen around. 'When my dad died, I couldn't bring myself to shut down the Haven Files admin on his website, so messages get routed to my in-box.' She joined him on the bed, moving stiffly, hoping he wouldn't notice. She could smell his soap, and when he shifted the laptop onto her lap, his fingers grazed her thigh.

It was the first time a guy had ever touched her. And even though it was accidental, she got a small thrill.

The message had apparently come through the contact form on his website – it was addressed not to Jake but to the administrator. It was written in all caps.

WHEN JESUS DIED, THE CURTAIN IN THE TEMPLE
WAS TORN INTO TWO PIECES. THE GRAVES
OPENED, AND MANY OF GOD'S PEOPLE WHO HAD
DIED WERE RAISED FROM DEATH. MATTHEW 27:51–3
GOD TURNS HIS FACE FROM ABOMINATIONS

AND CASTS MONSTERS DOWN TO HELL AND THOSE WHO DISOBEY HIS WORD WILL FEEL THE WRATH OF ETERNITY. AT HAVEN DEAD MEN WALK FROM THEIR GRAVES AND GOD DEMANDS JUSTICE FOR THE CRIMES OF THOSE WHO DON'T LISTEN. I WILL BRING HELLFIRE TO HAVEN LIKE GOD DID TO THE SINNERS AT BABYLON TO PURGE THEM FROM THIS EARTH AND I WILL BE WELCOMED BY ALL THE ANGELS IN HEAVEN WHO WILL SING MY PRAISES.

The message was signed *Angel Fire* and included a link to a Tumblr, www.wrathofgod.tumblr.com, but when Gemma tried to click on it, she found it disabled.

Jake took the computer back from her. 'The site was registered to an Estelle Williams in Sarasota. They already wiped it clean, but I managed to get screenshots, though. Give me a second.'

Gemma thought of all the pages she'd Googled turning up suddenly wiped or just failing to load. 'Who's they?'

He shifted on the bed, and Gemma realized he was nervous. 'One of the federal departments, I assume,' Jake said, looking at her sideways, as if expecting she wouldn't believe him. 'I wouldn't be surprised if by tomorrow everyone's reporting that Haven never existed at all – it was some holographic experiment and we're all supposed to forget about it. Look.' He swiveled the screen toward her again. 'This is some of Angel Fire's stuff.'

Gemma keystroked through a few pages, most of them decorated with grinning skulls or licks of flame and peppered with biblical verse and lots of exclamation points. 'She thinks they're raising people from the dead at Haven?' she asked.

'She *thought* that,' he said quietly. 'If she really is responsible for what happened, if she did turn herself into one gigantic IED, like they're saying, she's scattered across the marshes by now.' He shook his head, and Gemma couldn't help but think: another person dead. Another person dead because of Haven. Nurse M, Jake's father, and now this woman, Angel Fire. 'She must have timed her message to go out to a bunch of people at once. Even the news channels got wind of it, and they're always the last to know anything.' He closed the laptop and slipped it into his backpack – which was, predictably, black – and stood up. 'So? Are you ready?'

'I guess so.' She knew it was stupid to be freaked out by some nutter's theory about Haven and its weird science. But she couldn't shake the image of people staggering through the darkness of the marshes, reaching for her with clammy hands.

'You need to be *sure* sure.' Jake stood up. 'We might get arrested.'

Suddenly, though, Gemma felt as if all those Sour Patch Kids were nails trying to claw back out of her throat. She had the sense that being arrested would be the best thing that might happen to them.

Jake had told her that several weeks after his father died, he'd woken up in the middle of the night, certain that someone had just shaken him awake. But he was in the room alone. Still, every few minutes he felt a phantom pressure on his shoulder, as though someone was tapping him.

'I know what you're probably thinking,' he'd said, a little too forcefully. 'But I don't believe in things like that. Spirits, voices from the grave. I'm not like my dad.'

Still, the impression of a *presence* wouldn't leave him. Every few minutes, there was a tap-tap on his shoulder. So he had stood up, walked down the stairs, and walked straight out of the house.

His mom had just returned from Las Vegas, where she'd been living doing God knows what, essentially refusing to recognize the existence of her son except in the occasional birthday message, usually an email sent a few days late. Within a month, she would be gone again, and Jake would move in with his dad's sister, a widow who'd never had children and never wanted any.

Guided by a certainty he could never afterward explain, he had walked the five miles to the Wahlee basin campsite where he and his father had set off so many times together, and found a rowboat pitted with rust, likely left there by a local fisherman. The whole time, he said, he could feel an occasional tap on his shoulder, like a kind of Morse code, telling him to go on.

He had no compass. No water. No supplies. And yet somehow that night, alone in the marshes, he knew exactly where to go.

Dawn was breaking by the time he saw a bank of spruce and knew he'd reached Spruce Island. The institute was hidden from view. He realized he must have rowed all the way around to the west side of the island, which was still undeveloped. The security was lighter, too. There was a fence, and guard towers, but at dawn they were abandoned.

And still the finger kept tap-tap-tapping on his shoulder.

He pulled his boat up onto shore, less than ten feet away from a downed tree that had taken down a four-foot section of the fence.

He was on the island less than ten minutes before he was caught, thrown to the ground by military-style guards, frog-marched across the island and out to the dock, where police were already waiting for him. He never went near the main buildings, had only the briefest glimpse of the white-walled institute and the people inside it.

But it was enough.

She looked around the room, wishing she didn't have the melodramatic feeling she was seeing it for the last time. Even though it had been her idea to try and get to Haven tonight – or maybe because it had been – she felt she couldn't back out now. 'I'm sure,' she said, grabbing the only sweatshirt she'd brought. She wished it weren't bright pink.

Jake was obviously thinking the same thing, because he frowned. 'Take this.' He wrestled a black Windbreaker out of his backpack. It was a warm night, but the mosquitoes on the marshes, he told her, were killer.

Jake's car was so old it seemed predominantly composed of duct tape and string. 'Sorry,' he said, with an apologetic smile that made Gemma's heart purr. 'But at least you're getting door-to-door service.'

The car rattled so hard when he accelerated she was sure she was about to be expelled from her seat, that the car would just roll over and give up, panting, like a tired dog, but she didn't want to complain, and sat there white-knuckling her seat so hard her fingers ached.

'Just a few more miles,' Jake said. They'd looped around to approach Wahlee from the north, on one of the few roads that gave access to the nature reserve, and the bouncing of the headlights made Gemma feel seasick.

Miraculously, they made it without incident, although

Gemma could have sworn that the car gave a relieved sigh when Jake cut the engine. Stepping outside, she was immediately overwhelmed by the sound of the tree frogs. They were so loud and so uniform they seemed like a single entity, like the heartbeat of the world rising and falling. Even here, she thought she detected a faint smell of smoke.

Jake removed a flashlight from his backpack and gestured for Gemma to follow him. The Wahlee Nature Reserve was technically closed at sunset, and theirs was the only car. They moved onto one of the paths that cut into a thicket of pine and mangrove trees, and immediately Gemma felt a difference in the ground, a sponginess that made her heart turn over a little. Jake had told her casually that all the islands and marshes around here would be gone in twenty years, swallowed up by water. She imagined the trees submerged, stretching ghostly fingers up toward a sun filtered through layers of murky water. She wondered what April would think now, if she knew that Gemma was following a boy she didn't know into a darkened nature reserve with no one around for miles.

She didn't know anymore whether she was glad or worried that she hadn't told anyone where she was going.

They walked for fifteen minutes, though it felt like longer, and the sticky, humid air seemed to get all tangled up in Gemma's lungs. After a certain point they didn't seem to be following a path at all, and she had no idea how Jake was sure that he was heading in the right direction. The marshes had tides that shifted subtly and without sound: the water wouldn't even warn them before appearing suddenly beneath their feet. Jake stopped and touched her elbow.

'We're close,' he said. 'Go carefully. There are tidal pools here.'

'Okay,' Gemma said. Her voice sounded strange in the humid darkness, like it was being muffled by a pillow. She was sorry when Jake took his hand away.

A few paces farther on, Jake stopped completely and angled his flashlight at a patch of ghostly white saw grass, running down to a black expanse she now recognized as an inlet. Partially concealed beneath a myrtle oak was a bright-red kayak, which he'd rented from a local boat shop and stashed earlier that night. It was skinny and long as a Popsicle. Gemma's stomach dropped.

'I don't think we're both going to fit,' Gemma said desperately, as Jake bent over to drag the kayak free of the growth.

'Of course we will. It's a two-seater.' He pointed with the flashlight. There were, in fact, two seats in the kayak – if you could call them seats. Gemma thought they looked like those car seats meant for toddlers.

*I'm not going to fit,* Gemma wanted to say. But of course she couldn't. Not to him. Jake was the kind of guy who had size-zero girlfriends who modeled locally and were always complaining about trying to find clothes small enough.

'Can't we get another boat?' she asked desperately. 'A *boat* boat?'

He must have thought she was kidding, because he only laughed.

'Anything bigger will just get stuck. Some of the channels out there are so narrow even the kayak's a stretch.' Jake bent down and shoved the kayak down into the water, which sucked at the plastic with a wet farting sound. He steadied it with a foot. 'Besides, it's more comfortable than it looks.'

He clambered easily into the kayak – or the floating Popsicle – and somehow enfolded his long legs inside it, as if he were just sitting down in a chair. Then he maneuvered the kayak so he could reach out a hand to help Gemma inside.

'Come on,' he said. 'You'll be fine.'

She bit her lip. She had a sudden vision of getting stuck in her seat, of having to be hauled out of the kayak by a crane. Or worse, of not being able to fit inside in the first place. But she took his hand. As soon as she placed a foot into the kayak, it began bucking like a badly trained horse, and if the boat hadn't still been rooted in the mud of the bank, she was sure the whole thing would have gone over.

'All right, now the other foot . . . there you go, easy now . . .'

Somehow she managed to climb in without flipping the kayak, and even more miraculously, managed to squeeze herself down into the hard plastic seat, feeling a little like an elephant in a girdle.

'See?' Jake used a plastic paddle to push them out of the mud and turn them in the right direction. He was smiling at her again, his teeth white in the moonlight. 'Not so bad, is it?'

'For the record,' Gemma blurted out, 'this is *exactly* as comfortable as it looks.'

'Aw, come on. Don't be a baby.' But he was still smiling. And as they began to move through the marshes, her spirits lifted. Jake had given her a paddle but instructed her not to use it, and she was happy to let him do the work. They progressed steadily and in near silence except for the slurping of the water on the paddles. They'd agreed in advance that they should try and avoid talking as much as possible, in case there were patrols on the marshes.

So far it seemed their gamble – that after what had happened, security would be trying to get everyone out, not worrying about people trying to get in – was correct.

Occasionally helicopters passed in the distance on their way to and from the island, but less frequently now. And Gemma knew they must still be ferrying people *from* the island. It was unlikely, however, that given Haven's security, any survivors had even *made* it onto the marshes, which explained why they were putting hardly any effort into searching for them.

After an hour they'd met no one, heard no one, although occasionally they seemed to hear shouting in the distance, and Gemma knew they were still quite far from Haven. The marshes really did look like a labyrinth, full of narrow channels that forced them back toward the mainland before they could find another vein of water to follow in the right direction. Every few minutes, Jake stopped to consult the compass on his phone. With the saw grass growing as high as a tall man and mangrove trees furry with overhanging moss, they would have otherwise had no way of knowing where the mainland was and which way led to open ocean.

But there was a strange beauty to the marshes, and the tangles of dark weeds that drifted just below the surface of the water and came up on Jake's paddle, like long, dark fingers drawing him back, and the saw grass painted white with bird guano. The moon was full and bright, even behind a wispy covering of smoke, and so close Gemma could see individual craters, a pattern of trenches and shadow that made a grinning face. Jake picked out constellations to show her, and Gemma thought they all looked like they were winking down at her, letting her in on some secret. Jake obviously loved the marshes, despite what had happened to his dad here, and he told her stories of camping trips and frog-hunting expeditions, how his dad had renamed all the stars he didn't know and claimed Orion's Belt had been named for a drunk god who liked to pee in the Wahlee. Jake shook his head. *I believed him for so many years.* He smiled. *Whenever I see Orion's Belt, I think of him.*

It occurred to Gemma that this was the second time in the past twenty-four hours she'd been squeezed next to a cute boy in a strange vehicle. Maybe tomorrow she would meet a tall, dark, handsome stranger who'd want to take her on a motorcycle ride. Maybe she'd end up in Vegas working for the mob as a professional blackjack dealer.

At that moment, anything at all seemed possible.

She lost track of time completely but knew they must be getting closer. Sometimes she thought she heard the echo of overlapping voices, and once Jake froze, sticking the paddle down into the mud and shoving them into the shadow of an overhanging sand oak. But the voices always receded. If there were other people out in the darkness, the marshes were expansive enough to keep them at a distance.

At one point, Jake fished out his phone to check the

time and Gemma saw that he looked exhausted. She felt horrible: she hadn't been helping at all, and he'd been paddling for nearly two hours.

'One a.m.,' he said. He was a little out of breath. 'We must be getting close.'

'You need a break,' Gemma said.

'I'm okay,' Jake said, completely unconvincingly.

'You're a terrible liar,' Gemma said firmly. 'You need a break.' She, too, needed to stretch. Her feet had gone numb hours ago.

He didn't argue again. He angled the kayak up into the shallows and freed himself, so tired he didn't even complain when he sank a leg shin-deep in the mud. He helped shove the kayak onto sturdier ground so she could disembark. A rush of sudden feeling invaded her legs and she nearly stumbled. Jake caught her and for a second she was close to him, his hands on her elbow, his lips bow-shaped and his jaw just stubbled with hair and his eyes unreadable in the dark. She quickly pulled away.

She helped him haul the kayak farther into the grass so it wouldn't drift away. The saw grass grew nearly to shoulder height, and Gemma was glad, now, for the Windbreaker: it was sharp, and left sores on her exposed skin. As they hacked through the grass, for the first time in hours she spotted Spruce Island, by this point so close she could make out individual trees, and the spiky points of the guard towers, which looked to be abandoned. They had somehow come around the westernmost tip of the island, which was densely overgrown. She could make out none of the buildings, although some lingering smoke indicated a point in the distance where they must have been.

Gemma was so tired she'd forgotten to be nervous. Now, however, she remembered. 'What now?' she whispered. 'Do you think we can still get – ?' She broke off before she said *closer*. Jake went very still.

They'd both heard it: a muffled cry.

Jake grabbed her arm and pulled her into a crouch. He brought a finger to his lips, but there was no need. Gemma was so frightened, she couldn't have made a sound if she wanted to. The silence was anything but reassuring. They'd heard a voice, a human voice, ten, twenty feet away in the marshes. Which meant that whoever had cried out was now deliberately being quiet. Creeping up on them, maybe. Waiting to attack. Gemma pictured herself handcuffed in a military facility, a single lightbulb swinging overhead, an ugly army sergeant with a face like an old baseball mitt leaning forward to spit on her.

She was scared of Chloe DeWitt, ninety-pound blond shrimpoid. She would never make it in prison.

Then again, maybe she'd just get shot in the back, hit by a sniper from a distance of a hundred yards. One breath in and one breath out and then darkness forever.

Then they heard it: a faint rustling of the grass, followed by a sharp silence, as if someone had taken a step and then frozen. Jake was so still she couldn't even tell if he was breathing. The footstep had come from somewhere behind them. Jake gestured in the opposite direction. *Move,* he mouthed, and despite the fact that Gem's legs felt stiff and fatter than usual, she began to inch forward, shuffling crablike as quietly as possible. Her thighs were burning and tears sprang up unexpectedly in her eyes. Pathetic. Out here on the marshes in the middle of the night, crying because no one knew where she was, because she hadn't told her mom she loved her, because she hadn't told April, either, because her thighs were really out of shape and she would never wear a bathing suit again. . . . They would kill her, they would shoot first and make it look like an accident. . . .

'Who's there?'

The voice was harsh, male, and came from no more than ten feet behind her.

Gem forgot to stay down, forgot to stay quiet, forgot to keep hidden. Something screamed through her chest and into her head, an ancient voice shouting *go,* a force exploding into her muscles and lifting her to her feet. She was running. She was plunging blindly through the saw grass and the salt-eaten shrubs, ignoring the cuts on her shins and forearms. There were shouts, now, from all around her, or so it seemed – she didn't stop, wasn't thinking, couldn't hear anything but that drumbeat of panic.

Her foot snagged and her ankle went out. She stumbled on something buried in the grass and for a second that seemed like an eternity she was in the air falling, still imagining hands to reach out and grab her. She landed so hard the wind went out of her and she curled in on herself, shocked and airless, fighting for a breath that wouldn't come. Then Jake was next to her again, pulling her up so she was sitting. She finally took a breath, a long gasp of it, and began coughing.

'Jesus,' he whispered. He was sweating. He looked like he was going to be sick. 'Jesus Christ.'

'That voice,' she managed to say. 'Where did it come from? Where are they?'

'I don't know,' he said. 'Christ, Gemma. *Look . . .*'

She turned to see what had tripped her. Time that had moved so slowly seemed to crack entirely. For a long second she didn't understand what she was seeing, and then she thought – wished, hoped – it was an animal, some kind of strange underwater speckled thing, but then Jake drew back and began to cough, half choking, and dropped his flashlight: Gemma saw in its beam the dimpled elbow, the fingers curled in a half fist, and a green medical bracelet strapped around the bony wrist.

She couldn't have said, then or afterward, what made her reach out to part the grasses with a hand so that she could better see the girl's face. Instinct, maybe, or shock.

She was thinner than Gemma, much thinner. Her scalp was shaved, but in places a fuzz of brown hair had begun to regrow. Her green eyes were open to the sky and her mouth was open too, as if in a silent scream. There were four freckles on the bridge of her nose, four freckles Gemma knew because she counted them every day in the mirror, because Chloe DeWitt had once taken a pen and connected them during naptime in kindergarten. The soft plump mouth that had been her grandmother's. The hard angular jaw that belonged to her dad.

Behind her, Jake was still gasping. 'What the hell? What the hell?'

The girl — the dead girl — was wearing Gemma's face.

# NINE

GEMMA SOMETIMES HAD NIGHTMARES WHERE she was trapped in a crowd in an underground vault. In her dreams she was usually looking for someone, often her parents, sometimes April or even Rufus. But everywhere she turned she saw reflections of herself, not in mirrors but in the distorted faces of the people looking back at her, all of these not-Gemmas laughing the more frantic she became. She always woke up shaken and sick.

This was like that, only worse. She had the impression of swinging over a pit, as if the world might simply buck her into nothingness, and she would drown next to the dead girl who could be her twin.

She hadn't seen the stranger approach, hadn't noticed her at all, until she spoke.

'Cassiopeia?' She was extremely thin, not the kind of Chloe DeWitt thinness that came from weight-loss shakes and detox juicing and SoulCycle, but true, not-enough-to-eat, maybe-dying-of-cancer thinness. It made her bones stand out in her cheeks, her knuckles huge and mannish, her knees like sharp kites angling for a wind. Her head was completely shaved. Above her right eyebrow was a long white scar the width of a needle.

The stranger took an uncertain step forward and nearly tripped over the girl lying dead in the mud, and she drew a sharp breath and stopped, holding herself very still. When she looked up at Gemma, her face had changed. Gemma had the impression of huge eyes sunk in that narrow face, and a question in them she didn't know how to answer. She took in the girl's clothing – a white T-shirt, streaked with mud and grass and what looked like bird shit, ugly cotton elastic-waist pants – and then the girl's breasts, braless, hardly more than two sharp nipples beneath the fabric, her bare feet, the toenails colorless. Bare feet. Where had she come from with no shoes? But Gemma knew, even before she spotted the hospital bracelet, identical to the one secured around the dead girl's wrist.

'Oh my God.' She felt as if her heart had been stilled with a hammer. She pictured it like an old-fashioned clock, splintered into uselessness. 'I think – I think she's one of them.'

The Haven girl looked suddenly ferocious. 'Who are you?' she said. 'Where did you come from?'

'Who are *you*?' Jake's face was the bleached white of bone, but his voice was steady. Gemma wanted to reach out and take his hand. But her body wasn't obeying her correctly, and just then she was distracted by movement behind the girl, and something tall and dark and shadowed resolved itself into a boy.

'Lyra,' the girl said, and, when they said nothing, made an impatient gesture with one hand. 'Number twenty-four.'

'Oh my God,' Gemma said again. Her voice sounded high and shrill and unfamiliar, as if it were being piped through a teakettle. Her mind kept reeling away from the dead girl lying not four feet away from her, the pattern of freckles on her face, the exact shape of her mouth, reeling away from the truth of it, like a magnet veering away from its pair. 'There's another one.'

She knew the boy must be from Haven, too, as soon as he appeared. He was barefoot, and very thin, though not nearly so thin as the girl. Muscles showed through his T-shirt when he moved. He was mixed race and very beautiful, but there was something hard about him, too. He looked like one of the wax figurines in Madame Tussauds, where she'd gone with her mom on a trip to New York ages ago. As if you could stare and stare into his eyes and get nothing back. A person a little like a black hole: all the light vanished around him.

She didn't see the knife in his hand until the boy stepped forward so that the light showed on its blade.

'Look.' Jake put up both hands, as if he could physically stop the boy's progress. 'Hold on a second. Just hold on.'

The boy gave no sign of having heard. 'Who are you?' he said, keeping the knife high. Gemma realized in that second how stupid they'd been, how unprepared. They'd been scared of being arrested for trespassing. Not for a second had they considered that the Haven patients might be dangerous. Maniacs. Brain-altered killers. God only knew what kind of sick experiments they were doing there.

'We're nobody,' Jake said. Very slowly he reached down and helped Gemma to her feet. Her body felt dull and even heavier than usual, as if it belonged to somebody else. Now, standing, she had a clearer view of the dead girl who looked like her, and it was terrible, worse than any nightmare, like staring into an open grave with a mirror at the bottom of it. She thought she might fall. She hardly trusted her legs to carry her. Jake was still talking, but she could barely understand him. 'Listen, we're not going to hurt you, okay? My name's Jake Witz. This is Gemma. We got lost in the marshes, that's all.'

The girl frowned and turned to Gemma. Gemma was glad for the excuse to look somewhere, anywhere other than the body at her feet. 'But who made you?'

Gemma was sure she'd misheard. 'What?' she whispered.

'Who made you?' the girl repeated, more slowly this time, as if Gemma were very young or very stupid.

The wind, which had filled the marshes with a kind of constant, sibilant hiss, an underlying rhythm, went still. Gemma could feel the pressure of a thousand invisible eyes peering at her from the mud, from their many hiding places. 'I – I don't understand.'

'You're a replica,' the girl said.

'A *what?*'

'A replica,' she repeated impatiently. 'An organism descended from or genetically identical to a single common ancestor.' Gemma closed her eyes, hit with the sudden memory of being with her mom as a child at an art auction, bored out of her mind, listening to the auctioneer drone on and on about a vase that was supposedly the *exact replica* of the one in Versailles where Louis XVII had occasionally stored his false teeth. *Why*, her mother had leaned down to whisper, *would anyone spend so much money on a fake?*

'A clone,' she said. The word had a stupid, sci-fi sound to it. 'She means a *clone*, Jake.'

Jake winced. 'Yeah, well. I kind of already had that impression.' He kept his eyes on the boy with the knife.

Gemma felt panic pressing on her from all sides, from *inside*, as if thousands of tiny fists were beating inside of her to get out.

*A clone. A replica. Why would anyone spend so much money on a fake?* Gemma's thoughts were whirling like a hard snow, then disintegrating when she tried to catch hold of them. 'But – but it's impossible.' She knew she was hysterical, she knew she was loud, but she didn't care and couldn't help it. 'It's impossible. The technology doesn't exist; it's illegal. . . .'

'It's not impossible,' the Haven girl said. Gemma had the sudden, vicious urge to punch her, to take her huge eyes out of their sockets, to get her to stop speaking, stop staring, *stop*. 'At Haven, there were thousands of replicas.'

'Jesus,' Jake whispered. He closed his eyes for a second, and she saw that he looked almost restful. Peaceful. As if they hadn't just stumbled on a *girl with Gemma's exact face*, her chest black with blood; as if they hadn't found two survivors of the place, looking scared but also dangerous, like wild animals. '*Clones*. It all makes sense now.'

'Are you crazy? *Nothing* makes sense.' Gemma's heart was twitching like a dying bug. 'There's a *dead girl* with *my face* on her.' Jake turned to her, looking stricken, as if she'd reached out and slapped him. She wished she had.

She had the urge to slap him, to shake him, to shake the whole world and force it right again, like how her dad smacked the cable box whenever service was coming in weird. Thinking of her dad, of her home, suddenly made her feel very young and very afraid. She wished she'd listened to her parents. They'd been right all along. She should never have come. She wasn't strong enough.

'We're standing here in the middle of the fucking night and these – these people are telling me that there are clones running around out there, thousands of them –'

'Gemma, calm down.' Jake put a hand on her arm. She nearly screamed. But she was afraid to open her mouth again – afraid of losing it completely.

Her father had known about Haven. All this time, he'd known.

'Everyone needs to calm down, okay?' Jake was saying. The boy with the knife had tensed up again. 'Can you put that thing down, please? We're not going to hurt you.' The boy lowered the knife, finally. Jake had said the right thing, but Gemma didn't care. Even though they were standing in open air, she felt the sky might at any second collapse and bury them. She kneaded her chest with one hand, willing her heartbeat to slow down. The girl, she noticed, looked sick also. Somehow this made her feel less afraid. They couldn't be *that* dangerous, even if they did have a knife and look like creepy escaped psych inmates from a horror film. And when the girl couldn't stand anymore and instead crouched and ducked her head between her knees, breathing slowly, obviously trying to control her nausea, Gem felt sorry for her, and annoyed at the boy with the knife. He barely glanced at her.

She took a deep breath. 'What's the matter with her?' No one answered.

Without really intending to, she moved slowly toward the girl. When the girl shuddered, her spine stood out, almost architectural beneath her shirt, and for the first time in her life Gemma was actually happy she wasn't thin. She bent over. Her hand, as it floated toward the girl's shoulder, looked like a foreign object, a balloon or a spacecraft. 'Are you okay?'

For a millisecond she was surprised by the feel of the girl's warmth, the tautness of her skin and the muscle beneath it. The girl looked so insubstantial, Gemma had almost expected a hand would pass through her. Then the girl jerked away and Gemma took a quick step backward, her breath catching. The girl had looked at her with something close to hatred, and Gemma was again reminded of an animal – once a few years ago one of their handymen had cornered a rabid raccoon on the property and her father had taken out his rifle to shoot it, and she'd never forgotten how its eyes looked, desperate and wild, before the bullet hit.

'Maybe she's hungry,' Jake said.

The girl said nothing – she wrapped her arms around her knees and dropped her head again, her spine rising and falling with every breath – but the boy took a step forward. 'You have food?' His face was so full of open need that Gemma felt another lurch of pity. Had they been starved at Haven?

Jake squatted to rifle through his backpack. 'Sorry,' he said, producing a few granola bars and two bottles of water. 'We didn't bring much.'

The boy ate in a way that reminded Gemma of a squirrel, holding the granola bar with two hands and chewing quickly until it was all gone. He took water and drank half a bottle before passing it over to the girl, still crouching next to him. He said something too low for Gemma to hear, but the girl took the water from him and drank, and immediately she looked a little better. She would be very beautiful, Gemma thought, if she were heavier, if the lost, dark look of her eyes could somehow be warmed.

Jake couldn't take his eyes off them, the boy and the girl, and Gemma could hardly stand to look at him. She guessed that for him this was the end of a long mystery, the final act. For her this was the start. Her old world had exploded and she'd been born again into a new one. All she wanted was to go back.

'Look,' Jake said to them. 'I know you must be tired – you've been through – I don't even *know* what you've been through . . .'

Gemma thought she knew what he wanted, but hoped she was wrong. 'Jake, no,' she said warningly. She pressed a hand to her forehead, trying to push back the drumbeat of a migraine that was beating dully somewhere behind her eyes.

'They've been living in Haven, Gemma,' Jake said quickly, as if she hadn't understood. 'My father died for this. I need to know.'

'Jake, *no*.' The migraine exploded into existence: she imagined some sicko with a hammer pummeling her brain. 'I don't believe you. I literally don't believe you. These poor people have been through God knows what – they're starving and cold and they have no place to go – and you want to *interview* them –'

'I don't want to interview them. I want to understand.'

'Not people.' The girl spoke up unexpectedly. Gemma turned to face her.

'What?' she said. The girl was holding the water bottle tightly, her knuckles standing out. But she seemed calm.

'We're not people,' she said. Her voice had a low, musical quality, but it was strangely without affect, as if she hadn't been taught to feel or at least to express herself. 'You said, "These poor people have been through God knows what." But we're replicas. God didn't make us. Dr. Saperstein did. He's *our* God.'

All of Gemma's anger evaporated in an instant. She was alone momentarily in the dark with this thin, frail girl, this *clone*, who believed she was not a person. Gemma wanted to hug her. She wanted to understand, too – how she had become this way, how she had been made and why, who had taught her that God was out of reach. And she knew then that Jake was right, in a way. All the answers she needed, all the mysteries of her past, were bound up in the girl and boy from the island. She was still afraid of them, but also afraid for them in a way she couldn't verbalize. But she couldn't leave them alone. They had to stay close.

'We should camp here for the night,' she heard herself say, before she even knew that she was going to suggest it. Jake looked at her as if she'd lost her mind. Maybe she had. 'We'll go back to Wahlee in the morning.'

The boy seemed uncertain. 'We're not going anywhere with you.'

'No,' Gemma said evenly. 'No, you don't have to go with us. Not unless you want to.'

Once again, Jake just stared at her, as if a hand had just emerged from her mouth and started waving.

'Why would we want to?' the boy asked.

Gemma ignored Jake, speaking directly to the boy. 'You can't plan on staying here forever. You have no money. No ID. You're not even supposed to exist. And there will be people looking for you.'

She would have known this even if she hadn't seen, earlier that night, the helicopters pass overhead for hours, even if she hadn't seen soldiers outfitted in riot gear patrolling the coast. If the girl was telling the truth – and Gemma had proof that she was, in the form of the corpse she could hardly stand to look at – and Haven had indeed been full of clones, there had to be a reason for all the secrecy, the protections, the confidentiality. It should have been a miracle for modern science. The scientists who'd perfected the process should have won Nobel Prizes. Everyone in the world should have known about it. And yet nobody did.

The question was: Why?

She knew that whoever was in charge wouldn't allow the products of his or her experiments to run free, not when those products could talk and think for themselves. She assumed the only reason that the girl and boy, the *replicas*, hadn't been found and taken into custody already was because of all the chaos. Probably they were still counting the dead and the missing. Staying on the marshes for any length of time was a huge risk. But Gemma sensed that the clones weren't ready to move yet, and she knew that she had to stay close to them, that the ember of truth was here, with them. She needed time to think and to plan.

She expected more resistance from Jake. But he only shook his head and said, 'We should try and get some sleep. We'll want to get off the marshes as soon as possible.' And the clones didn't argue anymore. They obviously didn't want to be too far from the food and water.

They moved to the far side of a contorted thicket of mangrove trees that blocked them from a view of the body. Gemma didn't want to camp so close to the dead girl. She couldn't stand to think of her, that face like her face hollowed out by hunger, the hair that Gemma sweated and toiled to keep straight shaved close to her fragile scalp. She had never been superstitious, but it felt like a bad omen, as if the fate of her double might wear off on her.

On the other hand, she didn't want to go far in the darkness, and the girl and the boy, the replicas, were exhausted. The replicas bedded down side by side, although Gemma noticed that they hardly spoke or even acknowledged each other. As if they each belonged two separate realities that only coexisted momentarily.

Jake fell asleep right away, using a rolled-up towel as a pillow and clutching his backpack as though it were a teddy bear. Gemma, however, lay awake long after even the replicas had fallen asleep. It wasn't just because she was physically uncomfortable – she was clammy and too hot; the whine of mosquitoes needled her; the ground was uneven and unpleasantly spongy; she was dirty and she was sure that she smelled – but because of an itchy, hard-to-name feeling *inside*, like the wriggling of thousands of ants under her skin, in her blood and her veins. She imagined the girl on the other side of the trees, the second-Gemma, coming to life again, slithering through the mud, reaching for Gemma's face with bloodied fingernails, reaching for Gemma's hair, demanding it back. . . . She had to sit up, stifling a cry of terror.

Someone had cloned her. It was the only explanation that made sense, but she couldn't accept it. Had her father known? Was that why he had left Fine & Ives, and ruptured forever with his business partner? Was that why he'd wanted Haven shut down? A scientist had taken a sample of Gemma's DNA when she was a baby and used it to make another Gemma. Except . . .

The dead girl wasn't just another Gemma. She had Gemma's DNA, her face and her freckles, but even now her insides were liquefying, her stomach bloating with gases. She'd had a different name, different memories and preferences, and a very different life. Two people built of the same material, but radically separated by experience and now by death.

Had her father known? Or had he only suspected?

Maybe during one of her many hospital stays as a baby, someone had stolen some tissue from her without her parents' knowledge. That must be it. There would have to be a black market for things like this, places on the internet you could go to buy kiddie porn and new livers and medical samples.

She knew that was nonsensical, though. What were the chances that her DNA had randomly ended up in the same research institute her father's company had helped fund?

She would never sleep. How could she, with that dead girl, that doubled girl, so close by? So many thoughts were turning in her head, she felt dizzy. She had to *know*. She had to understand this place, and what her father's connection to it had been. What *her* connection to it was.

It was much harder to get into the kayak without Jake there to steady her, and again she had a fear of turning over and getting stuck, like a banana in a too-tight skin. But she managed it eventually and, after flailing around with the paddle for a bit, loosed herself from the tangle of long grass and reeds and maneuvered into the dark, glassy water. She didn't even know how to read a compass, even though her phone must have had one. But she felt confident that she was sufficiently close to the island that she wouldn't get lost, and she even had the idea of tying her sweatshirt to the overhanging branches of one of the mangrove trees, so that she would be able to find her way back.

After only a few minutes, she regretted the decision.

Paddling was much harder than Jake had made it look. Her heart was soon thumping and her shoulders ached. And she had to keep angling into the shadows and sloshing onto miniature pockets of land to orient herself. Down in the water she could see nothing, not with the mangroves crowding her and the reeds tall and spindly and white as bone. After a little while, the water became scummy with a fine layer of trash from the island, not just ash but human things, old buttons and charred plastic pieces and even bits of paper. She found a laminated ID entangled among the reeds: the picture showed a grim-faced black woman and indicated low-security clearance. She pocketed it. Now the thudding of her heart had nothing to do with the effort of paddling.

She came around a bend and sucked in a sharp breath: there beyond another stretch of muddy water was the fence, and empty guard towers, and trees blackened by fire beyond it. She must still be on the side of the island that had never been developed, because she could see only one long building through the trees, a shed or a storehouse that appeared abandoned. She dragged the kayak onto the shore and set out through the reeds down the narrow beach, as frogs splashed noisily into the water to avoid her, keeping very low to the ground in case there were still soldiers patrolling.

Here in the shallows was even more garbage, accumulated trash frothing against the grass. She angled her phone to the ground as a makeshift flashlight. She found a small rectangular sign, the kind that hung on office doors, indicating the way to Storeroom C, whatever that was. Its plastic was melted at the edges, so the sign looked as if it were bleeding out. She saw bits of plaster and white things studded between the rocks that she realized with a surge of nausea looked like pieces of bone. There were occasional stretches of sticky-dark stains, blacker than shadow, that she knew must be blood. The explosion must have been tremendous. And then of course had come the wind, which had carried the smell of burning all the way to Barrel Key and blown the fire into a conflagration.

After five minutes the trees thinned and the smell of charred plastic and campfire and something sweeter and deeper and more unpleasant intensified. At last she could see buildings – or at least, a single building – huge and rectangular and stained with soot, its windows shattered so that it appeared to be staring blankly out over the water. She was shocked to see the fire still burning, glowing dimly inside the building so that the walls were turned the strange translucent pinkish glow of a heart. She dropped into a crouch when she saw movement, pocketing her phone. Dimly she heard people calling to one another, and saw as her eyes adjusted people outfitted in firefighters' rubber pants and heavy boots. As she watched, she realized they were in fact stoking the fire, keeping it going, keeping it under control. And she understood that they'd been charged with burning the rest of Haven down, to make sure there was nothing left. She could go no farther, not without risking being caught.

Although the firefighters must have been a thousand yards away, she still winced when she stepped backward and heard a sharp crack. Turning, she saw that she'd stepped on a framed photograph, further shattering the cracked plastic that encased it. She bent down to retrieve it but could make out nothing more than a blur of dark figures. She pocketed it anyway and moved down the beach again, back in the direction she'd come. She waited until she could no longer hear the people or see the glow of fire through the trees before fishing out her phone again for light.

She recognized the man in the photo, heavily bearded and wearing a lab coat, as Dr. Saperstein, the current Haven director, from a picture she'd seen on the internet. He was outside, squinting against the sun, and in the distance she recognized the building she'd just watched burning, although the photograph was taken at a different angle, as though from an interior courtyard. Behind him was a statue – *the* statue.

In her memories, indistinct as they were, she'd always assumed that the statue represented some kind of god, but now she saw it was a David-like figure, a mortal, one arm thrown to the sky, one arm reaching down as though to draw something from the earth. In the photograph she could just make out a strand of DNA, represented by ribbons of interlocking stone, beneath its hand. The man in the statue had the posture of God forming Adam from the dust. It was a statue meant to represent the people at Haven and the work they were doing, the way they formed life from the earth, the way they had taken over for God.

And she, Gemma, remembered it. It was her earliest memory. Which meant: she'd been here before.

*Made here.* The idea was there, lodged in her mind, before she could unthink it. Made, manufactured, like the weird veggie patty they served in the cafeteria in school. She felt wild, dramatic, desperate. She thought for a second she might simply sit down and refuse to move, just wait for the salt to eat through her and the crabs to pick apart her bones.

But no. A new idea struck her and this time it felt like salvation, like finding a rope in the middle of a freezing riptide – she *couldn't* have been made at Haven, not cloned like the girl and boy claimed they had been. Like her double must have been. She'd seen dozens of pictures of her mom in the hospital, clutching an infant Gemma to her chest, sweaty and exhausted-looking, just moments after birth. There was one of her parents together, and minutes-old Gemma red and swaddled in a yellow blanket, and another of a nurse with a bottle of champagne. It was obviously Gemma in the pictures. Even then she'd had soft curls of brown hair and a snub nose that made it look as if it were being supported by an invisible thumb.

She felt calmer. She could breathe again. She was being silly. She might have visited Haven with her dad. And although she associated the statue with the idea of a long stay, she knew she might have made that up, or confused Haven with another one of the hospitals she'd been to as a child.

It was just after five thirty – time to get back, although she dreaded the return, of getting close to that horrible other who would rot out here with no one to mourn or bury her. But already, long electric tentacles of pink were swimming up through the darkness from the horizon. She knew she had to wake the others. It was time to get off the marshes.

She removed the photograph from its broken frame, folded it, and pocketed it next to the laminated ID she'd found entangled in the weeds. She was almost tempted to leave the photograph behind – carrying it made her feel jumpy and also ashamed, as if it were contraband or evidence of a crime. And it was evidence, although she didn't know, hadn't yet figured out, exactly what the crime had been.

Paddling felt even harder on the way back. Her arms ached and the lack of sleep had taken its toll. She was thirsty and exhausted. Even as it was driven off by the rising sun, the darkness played tricks on her. She kept thinking she saw movement in her peripheral vision, kept whipping around, half expecting to see another bloodied version of herself, holding her paddle like a weapon, only to see nothing but an insect skimming the water or a bullfrog blinking at her between the rushes.

It was lucky that the sky was lightening or she might never have found her way back. She passed dozens of mangrove trees extending out over the water, many of them overhung with mosses that in the dark might have looked like her sweatshirt. But she made it back a little after six and was surprised to find Jake and both clones still asleep. She knelt next to Jake.

'Hey,' she said. He woke suddenly, and for a second as he was still enveloped in sleep, Gemma saw a look of terror seize him. He blinked and it passed. She wondered whether he'd been having a nightmare.

She didn't want to touch the others – she hadn't forgotten how the girl had jerked away from her. Instead she stood at a careful distance and called to them until the boy came awake with a start, on his feet and reaching for his knife before he was fully awake.

'It's okay,' Gemma said quickly, as his eyes slowly found focus. 'It's just me. Gemma, remember?' The boy wiped his mouth with the back of a hand. His chest rose and fell beneath his T-shirt, and again Gemma was struck by how beautiful he was, beautiful and strange and wild-looking, like a new and undiscovered species. She couldn't fathom that he'd spent his whole life behind a fence. He was the kind of person who looked like he should be sailing on open seas, or parachuting down a mountain.

The girl had come awake, too. She looked even sicker than she had the night before. Her skin was a blue, bruised color Gemma associated with frostbite. But she couldn't possibly be cold. Gemma was sweating.

'There are still men on the island,' Gemma said. 'They're burning what's left of Haven.'

'You saw them?' Jake stood up. His hair was messy and his eyes were slightly puffy from sleep, but he still looked like he could be in an ad. 'You got close?' She nodded, and he frowned. 'You should have woken me. It's not safe.'

'What do you mean, they're burning what's left of Haven?' The girl stood up unsteadily. She brought a hand to her eyes as if she was dizzy.

'Just what I said,' Gemma said.

'Then there's no going back?' The girl spoke so

quietly Gemma nearly missed it.

Before Gemma could answer, the boy said, 'There's no going back. I told you that. They'll kill us if they find us. One way or another, they'll kill us.'

The girl shook her head as if she didn't believe that, but she said nothing. Gemma wanted to know what he meant by that — *one way or another, they'll kill us* — and thought he was probably exaggerating. But they were running out of time. Even now she could hear the distant roar of a motorboat engine.

She made a sudden decision: the girl was sick and needed help. Food, water, somewhere to sleep. Somewhere to *hide*. And Gemma needed to understand who she was, and whether she and the boy were telling the truth about the number of clones at Haven, and what they were being used for. She needed to understand who the girl who had Gemma's face was, and how she'd come to be. Maybe she could even figure out what her father knew and what he didn't. 'We have to get off the marshes. There will be new patrols now that it's light. They'll be looking for survivors.' And for the dead bodies, she thought, to count them. 'Come with us, and we'll get you clothes, and hide you someplace no one will be looking for you. Then you can figure out where to go. *We* can figure it out.'

Jake shook his head but didn't object. She noticed, however, that when he looked at her, he seemed almost afraid. She wondered what he thought about her now, after their discovery of the body, and felt a small cold hand grip her heart. But she had bigger things to worry about.

'Okay.' It was the girl who spoke. The boy shot her a look, either surprised or irritated or both – Gemma couldn't tell. But he didn't argue. 'Okay,' she said, a little louder. 'We'll go.'

There was nothing to pack up, and no breakfast besides two granola bars, which Jake offered to the replicas. Gemma was, for maybe the first time in her life, not hungry. The roar of distant powerboats was growing louder and more constant. They'd be taking things off the island, files and equipment too expensive to burn. But at some point soon, bodies would be counted, and three would be found to be missing. Then the soldiers would come looking for them.

Gemma had no desire to approach the dead girl again, but she felt bad leaving her there, too, to be used as a nest for flies and picked apart by wild animals. She hoped that someone would at least give her a decent burial. She shoved aside the idea of her own face lying in a chilly morgue somewhere, the freckled chest she knew so well split from sternum to stomach. Before they left, Gemma fought her way back through the mangroves and took a picture of the girl, forever still, forever sightless. A beetle was tracking across her left ankle, and Gemma wanted to reach down and brush it off but was too afraid. She didn't want to feel the iciness of the skin that was hers. She had a stupid idea that the girl might come roaring back to life, grabbing Gemma's wrist, furious that her double had lived when she had died. She backtracked quickly, zipping her phone into a pocket: her ever-growing stash of evidence.

Neither the girl nor the boy knew how to swim, and she guessed that made sense, although it was strange because they'd lived only a few feet from the ocean – but of course, on the wrong side of the fence. They would take the kayak while Jake and Gemma walked or half swam. Jake stashed his backpack at the girl's feet, and Gemma added the Windbreaker Jake had lent her to the pile as well. She didn't care if the rest of her clothes got wet. But she needed proof of what she'd seen and where she'd been.

Jake kicked off his sneakers, tied the laces together, and slung them over one shoulder. He rolled up his pants legs and waded into the water.

Gemma kicked off her shoes too and followed him in. The water was the temperature of a kiddie pool after someone had peed in it. It smelled a little like pee, too, and Gemma knew that was just because of all the decay, the singed plant life and dead bugs and the fish. The footing was silt-soft and slippery. Jake had told her last night that there were alligators in the marshes, and cottonmouth snakes, too. Gemma prayed they wouldn't encounter any.

The going was very slow. Jake held his phone high to keep it out of the water and directed the replicas which way to point the kayak. In places Gemma and Jake managed to stick to the shallows, where the water was only shin-deep, and move more quickly, but often the water was waist high or deeper and it was like a huge, outstretched hand was halting their progress. They slogged forward as the replicas drifted behind them, scanning the sky for helicopters. The sun rose and soon they could hear the noise of boat traffic, and see it in the miniature waves kicked up in the water by the boats' distant passage. Gemma had never known you could be in the water and sweaty at the same time, but she was both, and dizzy from the heat and the effort and the fear. Her lungs felt like they'd been strapped and squeezed into too-tight leather, like they might burst at any second.

'I can't go on,' she said. She could barely get the words out. 'I need to rest.'

Jake turned around as if he was going to object. But one look at her and he just nodded. She must look horrible, red-faced, sweaty, soaked up to her pits. But she was too exhausted to care.

They sloshed up onto solid ground again. Gemma

wished Mrs. Coralee, her stupid gym teacher, could see her now. Wilderness Gemma. In the past twelve hours she'd paddled a kayak and hiked nearly two miles through a slog of swamp. She'd probably keel over and die of shock.

Gemma's legs were shaking, and she sat down immediately in the mud. The replicas followed, disembarking clumsily from the kayak. Jake helped them drag it up beneath the shade of a mangrove, and not a second too soon.

'Get down,' Jake said hoarsely. They crouched together, shaded by the network of moss-fuzzed branches, while a roar grew steadily above them and the water splintered into waves. Then a helicopter swept overhead, so close it drove the dirt up into Gemma's eyes and stripped the leaves from several branches. But they hadn't been spotted. That she was sure of. Luck.

Jake stood up. She could read the tension in his whole body, in the set of his jaw and shoulders. 'I think we can make it back to the car overland from here,' he said. 'We can't be far. Can you walk?'

Gemma nodded, even though her thighs ached and she was desperately thirsty.

'We'll have to leave the kayak,' Jake said. 'Dragging it will slow us down.'

'You'll lose your deposit,' Gemma said stupidly. She

was so tired she could think only that they'd get in trouble with the rental shop.

Jake helped Gemma to her feet again but tightened his hand on her wrist to keep her from pulling away. 'Gemma, I want you to understand something. We're in very big trouble.' He spoke in a low voice, so the replicas wouldn't hear, and he kept his tone neutral, pleasant, even, as if they were just discussing the weather. 'The people running Haven are very powerful. They're going to be extremely unhappy that two of their experiments are walking free. They're going to be tracking us. They might *already* be tracking us. I need you to understand that.'

'We can't just leave them on the marshes,' Gemma whispered back. Over Jake's shoulder, she could see the girl watching her. The fuzz of brown hair cropped so close to her head made her look like a baby bird. Gemma looked away, lowering her voice further. 'They're half-starved. They could have been abused, for all we know. You heard what she said about not being human. Who the hell taught her that stuff?' Gemma thought of her father grinning proudly in front of Haven and felt nauseous all over again. 'Besides, the girl is sick or something. Take a look at her.'

'That's another thing,' Jake said. His eyes were so dark they seemed expressionless. 'We don't know what's been done to them. They could be carrying diseases.'

'Carrying diseases?' Gemma repeated. She pulled away from him. She was still shaking. 'You make them sound like animals.'

'Gemma, think about it.' He caught her arm again before she could turn away. 'We don't know what they were doing in Haven. They weren't making clones for the glory of it.' So he'd already come to the same realization that Gemma had: If Haven's goal had been to successfully clone a human being, why all the secrecy? 'They could be testing toxins, or studying smallpox. The point is, we don't *know* what they were doing.'

Gemma knew he was right. But she saw no other way of getting at the truth. And she was angry – angry because he wasn't meeting her eyes, because he acted as if it was painful even to touch her now. She turned away from him. 'This is what you said you wanted,' she said. 'Your father spent his life studying Haven and now, now that you have the chance to *know*, you're too scared.'

'Of course I'm scared,' he said quietly. 'They killed my father, remember?'

Now, on top of her anger, she felt guilty – which just made her even angrier.

'I'll take them back on my own, then,' she said. It was ridiculous: she would never find her way back. 'I don't care what you do. You have your answers. You finished your little quest.' She knew she was being unfair, but she couldn't stop. She was dizzy, and so damn thirsty, too. 'Come on,' she said, a little louder, to the replicas, who were standing there looking uncertain. Even Gemma was surprised by how harsh her voice sounded. The boy looked startled, then sheepish, and, perversely, she felt a rush of pride: she'd scared him, the big baddie with the knife.

Jake caught up with her before she'd gone even two steps. 'Don't be stupid,' he said. To her relief, he didn't seem mad. Already she felt terrible. His father had *died*. 'We're in this together. Besides, no way am I letting you get all the credit.' His smile was strained, but at least he *was* smiling, and Gemma felt a wave of relief. She hadn't realized how afraid she was of losing Jake's help.

Jake took the lead again. He was right: they were able to make it back to the car on foot, circumnavigating the narrow veins of water, although he had to stop frequently to consult the compass and the GPS on his phone, once cell phone service patched in again. At some point the composition of the ground shifted subtly beneath their feet, but it wasn't until Gemma saw a *No Littering* sign that she realized that Jake had led them safely back onto the nature reserve. After another two minutes they were within sight of the car, and Gemma nearly shouted with joy. There was a case of bottled water in the trunk, and they each downed a bottle. It was, Gemma thought, the best thing she'd ever tasted.

They piled into the car. Gemma felt better once they were no longer standing in the open. In the car, they could be anyone. Picnickers, backpackers, sightseers, friends. The replicas, on the other hand, seemed very nervous. It occurred to Gemma they had likely never been in a car before, and the boy jumped when Jake turned on the ignition and the radio blared to life.

Gemma had been without cell service since they'd first paddled out onto the marshes, but as soon as they pulled back onto the dirt road that led to Wahlee, her phone came alive with texts, voice mails, and alerts, almost all of them from April.

She dialed April immediately, praying she would pick up.

'*Jesus*. You were supposed to call me ASAP. I thought you'd been dismembered by an ax murderer or taken to Guantánamo or something. What the hell happened?'

Gemma didn't know why, but hearing April's voice – so familiar, so *April* – made her want to cry. For the first time she let herself think that they were safe. They were okay. They were speeding along a dirt road toward civilization and fast-food burger chains and bad pop music and normal life. Being on the marshes had been disorienting, like a nightmare that keeps its hold on you even after you wake up. Except this time they'd pulled two people from the nightmare. They'd brought proof of its reality back.

She took a deep breath, blinking rapidly to keep the tears back, aware that Jake was watching her. 'It's a really long story,' she said. 'Did my mom call?'

'Only about seven times,' April said. 'I told her you ate bad sushi and were puking your brains out and then went to sleep. I'm telling you, Gem, you owe me major on this one. I'm talking free lunches for a month. Maybe a year. I'm talking vacation-to-Disney-World owe me.'

'Okay.' Gemma closed her eyes and leaned back against the headrest. The sun was warm on her face, and the air-conditioning smelled reassuringly of chemical exhaust. 'Listen. Did your grandparents leave for their health conference thingie?'

'It's not a health conference. It's a wellness retreat.'

'Yeah, whatever. But the house is empty for a few days?'

'Yeah.' April's voice had turned suspicious. 'Why?'

Gemma opened her eyes again. They were passing out of the Wahlee Park Reserve now and back into Wahlee. A cop car was parked by the side of the road, its lights circling noiselessly. The driver's seat was empty. She wondered where the cop had gone. She felt an itch on the back of her neck, like someone was dragging a fingernail there. Not safe. Not by a long shot.

'I'm going to need your help,' she said, gripping the phone so hard, it made her palm sweat. 'I made it all the way to Haven, April. And trust me. You might want to save your IOUs. This is just the beginning.'

'Holy shit.' There was a long pause. 'What did you find?'

'Not *what*.' In the rearview mirror, Gemma could see the boy's profile, elegant and dark. *'Who.'*

# TEN

GEMMA HAD BEEN HOPING THAT once they got to April's grandparents' house, she could install the replicas in the guesthouse before she had to answer any questions. She should have known, of course, that April would be watching from the front windows. She rocketed out of the door and onto the front lawn as soon as she saw Jake's car turn in the driveway.

'Gemma!' The force of April's hug nearly knocked Gemma backward. April pulled away, squeezing Gemma's shoulders. 'You look like shit. And' – she made a point of sniffing – 'you stink.'

'Nice to see you too,' Gemma said, but she was too tired to be offended. April smelled like suntan lotion and Coke.

April's eyes went to the car. 'Is that – I mean, are they in there?' Gemma nodded. April licked her lips. She was tan and relaxed-looking, her shoulders peeling, and standing next to her, Gemma felt a thousand years old. 'You're serious about . . . you think they're really clones? Real clones?'

'No, fakes,' Gemma said, and then saw that April was too distracted to catch sarcasm. 'Yes, real,' she said. 'At least, that's what they told me.'

'But you don't have proof,' April said, sounding almost disappointed. 'You haven't seen, you know, *doubles*.'

Gemma thought again of the body stretched out in the grass, a body just like hers except so much thinner than her own. She hadn't told April about seeing the girl who had to be her clone, her replica. She wasn't ready for that. Not until she understood more than she did now. Instead she said only, 'I think they're telling the truth. Why would they lie? They were raised on that island. They were *made* there. They've been told they're less than human. The boy doesn't even have a name. Just a *number*.' That was what the girl, Lyra, had told them in the car.

April hugged herself. 'God,' she said. She was still staring into the car. Turning, Gemma was relieved to see that because of the direction of the sun, Lyra and 72 were no more than blurry silhouettes. She had a feeling that once word got out – which it had to, there would be no way to keep the truth secret now – they'd have plenty of people staring at them. 'Can I meet them? Is it safe to let them out?'

'They're not animals,' Gemma said, surprised by the harshness of her tone. April flinched, and Gemma felt instantly guilty. 'Sorry,' Gemma said. 'I'm tired. *They're* tired.'

April ignored that. 'And who's *that*?' Her eyes had landed on Jake. She looked as if she wanted to lick him. Gemma was surprised her tongue wasn't lolling out of her mouth.

'Look, let me just get everyone into the guesthouse, okay? And then we can talk, and I'll tell you everything.'

'You better,' April said, still staring at Jake. 'I've been covering your ass for days.'

'I know,' Gemma said. 'You're the best friend in the world.'

'Universe,' April corrected her.

They'd stopped at Walmart on the way to April's house and bought clothes, food, and toiletries with the credit card her parents had given her, trusting that they never reviewed the statements too closely – one of the few benefits of having parents who kept you on the world's tightest leash, and at least occasionally felt guilty about it. She was dying to ask both replicas about Haven, but the lack of sleep was catching up to her. She felt as if her brain had been replaced by sludge.

The guesthouse was cool and decorated in lots of beach pastels. The boy held himself very carefully, as if he was afraid to break something. Lyra stopped in front of the bookshelves, staring up at the old warped paperbacks, mass-market romances, and thrillers with time-smudged spines, as if she'd never seen books before. Maybe she hadn't. Gemma wondered whether she'd been educated, whether she knew how to read and that there were seven continents, that the earth orbited around the sun. So many questions, so many things she needed to understand.

'Get some sleep,' Gemma told them. She was feeling calmer since they'd made it to April's house without getting arrested or swarmed by SWAT teams or whatever. They were safe. They had time.

Jake and Gemma left the replicas to rest in the guesthouse. Gemma was exhausted, but as soon as they stepped outside, Jake – who had been quiet through almost the entire car ride – began to talk. 'You know what doesn't make sense to me?' he said. 'Why all the secrecy? People have dreamed of cloning humans for years. They've barely been able to clone animals. Most clones die early. The scientists at Haven should get the Nobel Prize. They should be on TED Talks. They should be billionaires, you know? So why haven't they told anyone?'

'I don't know,' Gemma said, as they skirted the pool toward the main house. The sun was dazzling off the water. She wished she had sunglasses. 'But Fine and Ives has military contracts, like you said. They always have. Maybe Haven was using the clones for drug testing. Isn't that what you thought they were doing out there, Dr. Whatever-his-name-is and his orphan charity and his human experiments?'

Clones no one knew about, no one cared about – they could be used as human guinea pigs. No wonder they'd been given numbers, not names.

It would explain, too, the fact that her father had known Richard Haven, had been photographed with him and spoken about his genius in interviews. It might explain his sudden change of attitude and abrupt departure from Fine & Ives right after Richard Haven's death, and just when Fine & Ives had begun to invest. Gemma could imagine her father excited by the idea of human cloning, by the scientific possibility of it, only to feel disgusted should it actually succeed. And no matter how horrible he was, she couldn't imagine that he would willingly get involved in testing deadly drugs or toxins on human beings, cloned or uncloned, without their consent. It had nothing to do with empathy. He simply liked rules too much.

Still, no matter which way she thought about it, her father must have known what was really going on at Haven. He'd known, and he'd turned his back on what was happening. He had retreated with his family to Chapel

Hill, hiding behind tall gates and manicured lawns and money. Despite what she knew about her father – his coldness, the way he hardly seemed to care about his own family – she couldn't believe it. How would she ever look at him again?

'Dr. Saperstein is the director of Haven. The Home Foundation is the name of the charity he founded,' Jake said evenly. 'But it doesn't make sense to do medical testing on clones. Clones are expensive to make. I mean, Haven has been paying for their care, feeding them, keeping them healthy – or at least *alive*. It seems like a lot of effort if they're just going to fill them up with drugs.'

He had a point. It was all too much. She suddenly felt like crying. 'Please,' she said. '*Please*, can we talk about this later?'

'Sure. Of course.' Jake squinted at her as if her face was a puzzle and he was trying to arrange it in the correct order. He looked like he was about to say more, so Gemma sped up to beat him into the house. Jake went off to take a shower – April, perv that she was, seemed *way* too interested in explaining how the faucet worked, as if expecting him to start stripping if she just gave it enough time – and Gemma took the opportunity to retreat to April's room and collapse onto the bed.

Gemma had never wanted to sleep more badly in her life. But as soon as she pulled out her phone, she saw more missed calls and texts from her mom. The last text had come in from her mom only fifteen minutes ago. *CALL ME*. She wanted to do nothing less, but she pulled up her home number and dialed.

Her mother picked up on the first ring. She'd obviously been waiting by the phone.

'How are you feeling?' Kristina asked.

'I'm fine,' Gemma said cautiously. She'd been expecting her mom to sound angrier.

'April said you were sick. I tried calling the house several times, *and* I've been calling your cell. . . .' Her mom's voice was edged with suspicion.

She'd completely forgotten April's cover story. 'I'm still really tired,' she said quickly. That, at least, was the truth. 'I've been basically sleeping since I got here.'

'Well, I'm glad you're feeling better,' she said. 'Listen, I've spoken to your father. He's very upset . . .'

Gemma's heart started beating harder.

'. . . but I've convinced him there's no reason to rush home,' Kristina finished.

Gemma exhaled. 'So he's staying in Shanghai?'

'He was already in London when I managed to reach him,' she said. 'He's going to stay there for a few days and take some meetings. But he wants you home by the time he gets back on Saturday. I'll email you some flight options later.'

It was better than Gemma could have hoped. It was Wednesday. That gave her almost a full three days. 'I was thinking I'd just drive home with April –' she said, but her mom cut her off before she could finish.

'Don't push your luck,' Kristina said, her tone changing and becoming harder. 'You'll fly on Saturday morning and we'll figure out how to manage your father.' Again Gemma felt that hard squeeze of anger, of hatred, bringing a burn to the back of her throat. 'And Gemma? I wouldn't try to call your dad just now. He's still quite upset.'

*I wasn't planning on it,* Gemma nearly said. But she thought she'd take her mom's advice and wouldn't push her luck. 'Okay,' she said. 'Love you, Mom.'

'You better,' Kristina said. She was smiling, though. Gemma could hear it in her voice. Maybe, Gemma thought, she and her mom would run away somewhere. To California. To Paris. Somewhere her father wouldn't be able to find them. 'Love you too.'

There was a tangle of discarded clothes and bathing suits on April's bed, but Gemma didn't bother clearing it off. Instead she crawled in under the covers, still wearing her jeans and T-shirt. She could hear the water gushing in the other room, but the thought of Jake showering – *naked*, so close by – no longer made her blush or feel much of anything. When her phone started ringing again, she picked it up without checking the screen.

'Mom,' she said, 'I'm going back to sleep for a bit, okay? I'm not feeling great.'

'Now that's a first.' It wasn't her mom on the phone, but *Pete*. She recognized his voice. 'I've heard *stud* before. *Babykins, hotcakes.* No one's ever called me *Mom* before.'

Gemma smiled, and her face nearly cracked. She brought a hand to her cheeks. Already it felt as if she hadn't smiled in days. 'I'm not buying it,' she said. 'No one's ever called you hotcakes, either.'

'Fair enough.' His voice changed. 'What's the matter? Are you sick? Or just missing me?'

She rolled her eyes before remembering he couldn't see her. 'You wish. Anyway, *you* called *me*. What's up?'

'Just checking in,' Pete said. 'I wanted to make sure you weren't lying in a gutter somewhere.'

'Barrel Key doesn't have any gutters,' Gemma pointed out.

'You know what I mean,' Pete said. 'Did you find whatever you were looking for?'

'More,' Gemma said. She closed her eyes, allowing herself to relax for the first time in twenty-four hours. April's bed was cloud-soft and smelled deliciously of lavender. 'Look, can I talk to you later? I really do need to sleep.'

'Big night, huh?' Although Pete's voice was still light, Gemma thought he sounded hurt. But she was too tired to explain. She closed her eyes and saw the dead girl again, and the beetle tracking across her ankle. She knew that the body bloated after death and imagined the girl balloon-like, distended, and quickly opened her eyes again.

'You could say that,' she said.

'Feel better.' He'd recovered quickly and was his usual, cheerful self. 'Stay away from the gutter, okay?'

'I'll try,' Gemma said. Before he could hang up, she added, 'Hey, Pete?'

'Uh-huh?'

'Thanks. Just . . . thanks.' Then she hung up before she could begin to cry. She rolled over, burying her face in the pillow. When she closed her eyes, she forced herself to focus on Pete's eyes, and the pale blond of his lashes; the crooked look of his smile and the way he sang along to the radio station, getting all the words wrong. But soon Pete's face was merging with Jake's, and Pete was frowning and dressed in all black, at a funeral for Gemma's father – except when she looked inside the casket, she saw her own face reflected, her own body stitched and sutured and gray beneath its garish makeup, her mouth open as though to scream.

She woke disoriented. Only when she saw that the sun was setting did she realize she'd been asleep for most of the day. She felt a hundred times better, clearer, more focused. For several minutes she lay in bed, letting her heartbeat return to normal, trying to ignore the shadow of the terrible nightmare that still clung to her, like a film of sweat.

Why did she have that stubbornly persistent idea that she'd been at Haven, stayed there for a long period of time? Could her father possibly have *allowed* the scientists at Haven to extract his only child's DNA, just so they could create her human double? Could he have been *using* her, maybe concealing the truth from her mom? It was a horrible idea, and she couldn't believe it, even of her father.

It was time to get answers.

In the bathroom she splashed cold water on her face and scrubbed her teeth with a finger before remembering she had a toothbrush in her backpack. She found Jake alone in the kitchen in front of his laptop. He got up when he saw her and then quickly sat down again. He was nervous, she realized. She was *making* him nervous. Was it because he felt sorry for her? Or was he afraid?

'Where's April?' Gemma asked, drawing a glass of water from the sink and drinking deeply. She felt as if she was washing away the taste of the marshes, still burned into the back of her throat.

'She went out,' he said, giving her a smile that could have launched a thousand memes. Strangely, though, it was Pete she wished for, Pete she wanted to see. Pete belonged to her life Before. 'She kept asking questions, but I wasn't sure what I should and shouldn't say. I think she got tired of me.'

He shrugged, and Gemma stopped herself from saying she doubted it. More likely, April had gone out before she could murder Jake by slow humping.

'Did you sleep?' he asked, and Gemma nodded. She nearly told him about the nightmare but didn't.

Gemma pulled out a chair and sat down across from him, cupping her chin in her hands. 'How about you?' she asked.

He shook his head. 'I've been running searches on the explosions, you know. Just trying to sort out what really happened.' He made a face. 'You won't believe this.'

'Try me,' she said. Twenty-four hours ago, she wouldn't have believed in clones, or that she'd paddle a kayak across an ash-strewn marshland to try and sneak onto what might as well be a military base, or that somewhere in the world there was a girl bearing her exact likeness. Now she thought she might believe anything.

'The woman who strapped herself full of explosives –'

'Angel Fire,' Gemma said, remembering the name from the message that had come in to the Haven Files.

He nodded. 'Right. Angel Fire. She left a backpack at Barrel Key. Maybe she camped there overnight, I don't know. And she had *every single page* of the Haven Files printed out and stashed in her backpack.' He looked vaguely nauseous. 'The website keeps crashing.'

A bad feeling worked at the bottom of Gemma's stomach, like someone had a fist around her intestines. 'That's not good, Jake,' she said. 'The police will come for you next.'

He laughed, but without humor. 'Already have. I missed two calls from some Detective Lieutenant something.'

'What are you going to do?' Gemma asked.

Jake started ordering things on the table, lining up edges, the way he'd done in the diner. A nervous tic, obviously. 'I'll be all right,' he said, although he didn't sound convinced. 'I had nothing to do with it, anyway. They can't pin anything on me.'

Gemma hoped he was right. 'You never told me what happened to Richard Haven,' she said.

Jake sighed and closed his laptop. For a split second, he looked much older. 'Killed,' he said simply. 'Only a few years after Haven was built. Car accident while he was on vacation in Palm Beach.' She remembered, now, reading something about Richard Haven's death, when she'd first been searching for information about the institute. Already it seemed like a different lifetime. 'Most Haven-ites don't think it was an accident.'

'Havenites?' Gemma repeated, and Jake blushed.

'Sorry,' he said. 'That's what the Haven groupies call themselves. My dad was the biggest Havenite of all.'

Gemma absorbed this. 'So it was murder? Another murder?' That would make Jake's father, Nurse M, whoever she was, and Richard Haven all victims of murder made to look like accidents or suicides instead.

'It was broad daylight,' Jake said. He leaned back in his chair. 'There was no rain, no bad weather, nothing. And from the way the car was positioned and the place it went off the road, it looked like Richard Haven must have swerved to avoid someone. But no one ever came forward.'

'But it doesn't make sense,' Gemma said. 'The other woman, the nurse who committed suicide —'

'Nurse M,' Jake said.

'Right. I mean, she was threatening to talk to the media, wasn't she? Your dad was supposed to *interview* her.' He nodded. 'I can understand why she'd be a threat. But Richard Haven founded the institute. He wouldn't have wanted it shut down or exposed or whatever.'

Jake rubbed his eyes. 'As far as we know,' he said. 'But that's the thing. We don't know. Richard Haven was in it from the beginning — before the military got their hands in it through Fine and Ives. Maybe he was having doubts. Maybe he wanted to back out of the whole agreement.

Or maybe he just decided he wanted recognition for his life's work. There could be a thousand reasons he became dangerous.'

Gemma absorbed this in silence. Outside the window, the sun had sunk below the rooftops, leaving only a smear of red behind, like a bloody handprint. She stood up. 'Come on,' she said. 'Time to wake up our sleeping beauties.'

The houses in this complex were nestled one right next to the other. From above it must have looked like a jigsaw puzzle of roofs and tiled pools and squat gardenia bushes. Gemma could smell someone grilling, and hear the blare of a television from a nearby house. It was weird to think of all those other people so close, fixing dinner or watching Netflix or worrying about their bills, totally unaware of the explosion that had punched through Gemma's life.

She felt very alone.

The guesthouse was dark. The replicas were still sleeping. Gemma could hear the boy snoring. She eased the door to the bedroom shut, figuring that if she wanted to get the truth about Haven she would need to start by buttering them up a little, earning their trust. She rooted around in the guesthouse cabinets until she found a pot.

'What are you doing?' Jake asked.

'Haven't you ever heard?' Gemma next began opening

the cans of chili she'd bought at Walmart. 'Fastest way to a person's heart is through the stomach.'

Jake smiled. 'Ah. Of course. That's why the police use so many cupcakes in their interrogations.' His hair had a funny cowlick, and for some reason it made Gemma sad. It was so *normal*. She knew she'd never feel normal again, not ever.

She had always joked about feeling like an alien, but she knew now that until today she'd had no idea what that meant.

'We're not interrogating them. We're talking to them. It's different.' The stove sputtered for several seconds before it lit. 'Turn on a light, will you? I can't see anything.'

The room flared into shape, blandly reassuring: seashell prints on the walls, a sign in the kitchen that said *This Way to the Beach*. Jake wandered over to the small antique roll-away desk, which was the only piece of furniture in the whole open-plan room that wasn't white or beach themed. Suddenly, he sucked in a sharp breath, as if he'd just seen a snake.

'What?' she asked 'What is it?'

He had picked up a manila folder, the kind Gemma associated with dental records. 'It's a medical report from Haven.' He looked up. His eyes were burning again with that dark light, the kind that seemed to absorb and not reflect. 'They must have brought it with them.'

He moved to the couch with the report and powered up his computer again. Gemma came to look. The folder was disappointingly light and contained only a single, double-sided report. Still, it was something. She leaned over and read from the heading. *Form 475-A. Release Authorization and Toxicity Report. Human Model 576.*

'What does it mean?' she asked. The whole report might as well have been written in another language. Every other phrase was one like *over-conversion* or *neural impairment* or some string of weird chemical-looking codes like vCJD-12 or pR-56.

'Let's ask the oracle,' Jake said. 'Google,' he clarified, when she looked at him.

She sat on the arm of the couch, because when she leaned any farther she was forced to inhale him, the new soap smell and the warmth of his skin, and she got distracted. But she felt awkward sitting there, posed and clumsy, like an overinflated doll, and so she returned to the stove just to have something to do.

When the bedroom door opened, she spun around, startled. Lyra looked better than she had on the marshes. Pretty, despite the sallowness of her skin and her cheekbones like beveled edges. But there was something frightening about Lyra's stillness, and the blandness of her facial expression, as if there was nothing inside directing her, as if she were hollow, like a puppet.

Gemma slopped some of the chili into a bowl. 'Here,' she said. Her voice sounded hysterical in the silence. 'Chili. From a can. Sorry, I can't cook. You need to eat.'

Lyra didn't thank her. She didn't say anything. She didn't even sit down. She just took the bowl from Gemma automatically and began to eat mechanically, holding the spoon wrong and the bowl to her lips and shoveling the chili into her open mouth. It was strange to see a girl so fragile eat like that, like she was actually a trash compactor. Weirdly, Gemma liked her better for it.

'Transmissible spongiform encephalopathies,' Jake said, and Gemma jumped. This was it: they were on the verge of understanding. Suddenly all her fear left her at once. It was like standing at the top of a really steep sledding hill and then letting go. There was nothing to do anymore but ride. 'That's a category of disease. Mad cow is a TSE.'

'Okay.' Gemma went to sit next to Jake on the couch again. It was better than standing next to Lyra, the living evidence of whatever deranged experiments they were doing at Haven. 'But what does that mean?'

'I don't know.' Jake rubbed his forehead as if he had a headache. 'There are just references to it in the report.'

At the sink, Lyra released her bowl with a clatter. Gemma looked up and saw she'd gone very still. 'You shouldn't be looking at that,' she said. Gemma wondered at Lyra's loyalty to Haven — was she trying to protect its secrets?

'Why not?' Jake turned to Lyra. 'You stole it, didn't you?'

'Yes,' Lyra said evenly. 'But that's different.'

'It's not like they'll miss it now. The whole place is an ash heap.'

'Jake,' Gemma said quickly. For the first time, Lyra had flinched.

He shrugged. 'Sorry. But it's true.' He didn't sound sorry at all. He sounded angry. And Gemma knew how he felt. If even a fraction of what they suspected of Haven was true, she was glad it had burned to the ground. She bent forward over the report again, trying to make sense of the baffling medical terminology and shorthand. Among the jumble of terms she couldn't understand, she spotted repeated references to Human Model 576, *generation seventeen, cluster yellow.* 'Lyra, do you know what these groups mean?' Gemma kept her voice light. Lyra was still motionless by the sink, as if she was waiting for someone to tell her what to do. Maybe she was. 'The patient — the replica, I mean.' She looked up, wondering whether she had used the term correctly. After a second, Lyra barely nodded. 'She was in the yellow cluster?'

'The Yellows died,' Lyra said. Gemma went cold.

There was something terrible in Lyra's matter-of-factness. 'There were about a hundred of them,' she went on, 'all from the youngest crops.' She could have been talking about anything. Groceries. The weather. Toilet paper. 'Crops are for different generations. But colors are for clusters. So I'm third crop, green cluster.' She held up her wrist, and Gemma saw the green hospital bracelet, truly saw it, for the first time. 'They must have made a mistake with the Yellows. Sometimes they did that. Made mistakes. The Pinks died, too.'

'They all died?' Jake asked.

Lyra nodded. 'They got sick.'

'Oh my God.' According to the report, Human Model 576 hadn't been even two years old when she died. 'It says here she was only fourteen months,' Gemma said, because somehow she needed to speak the words, to get them out of her chest where they were clawing at her. Not a specimen. A *child*. Small and fat-cheeked with little fists that wanted to grab at things. Gemma loved babies, always had. Who didn't?

'You said colors are for clusters,' Jake said slowly. 'But clusters of what?'

Lyra shrugged. 'There are different clusters. We all get different variants.'

'Variants of what?' Jake pressed, and Gemma almost didn't want to know the answer.

For a second, Lyra looked almost annoyed. 'Medicine,' she said, so sharply that Jake briefly glanced at her.

'Look, Jake. It's signed by Dr. Saperstein, just like you said.' She had the urge to take pair of scissors to it, to cut it into little shreds as if doing so would hurt the real person, too. Below Dr. Saperstein's signature – which was hard and angular and fit Gemma's impression of Dr. Saperstein as someone made all of angles and corners, someone from whom human feeling had been carved away – a nurse, Emily J. Huang, had signed as well.

'Dr. Saperstein is in charge of the growth of new crops of replicas,' Lyra said, and Gemma tried not to wince when she used that word, *crops*. She was surprised when Lyra voluntarily came closer. She didn't sit, but she hovered there. Maybe she *could* read. Her eyes were moving in the right way. Normally Gemma found people who read over her shoulder intensely annoying, but she was afraid of doing anything to startle Lyra away. 'He signs all the death certificates.' Gemma was surprised when Lyra smiled faintly. She reached out and touched Emily Huang's name with a finger – gently, as if it were something fragile, a ladybug or a butterfly. 'Nurse Em signed, too.'

*Nurse Em.* Something burst across Gemma's mind – an electric pulse of understanding. She leaned back and closed her eyes. She saw whiteness, as if she'd been staring at the sun, and silhouettes stumbling in front of it, chanting soundlessly to her. 'Nurse Em,' she said out loud, testing the sound of it. Yes.

'Holy shit,' Jake said, and she knew that he, too, had understood.

Emily J. Huang.

Nurse M.

# ELEVEN

GEMMA FELT CLAUSTROPHOBIC EVEN ONCE she
was outside. She'd felt in that small bright box of a living room as if the ceiling were going to collapse – for a
second she'd almost hoped it would. Now she knelt and
plunged her head into the pool, which was shockingly
cold, and came up gasping, her hair running water down
onto her sweatshirt. But still she sensed a terrible pressure all around her, as if an invisible hand was trying to
squeeze her into a sandwich bag. But she knew that in
fact the pressure came from inside, from the weight of the
truth and all that Jake had found out.

*Ask and ye shall receive.*

They had wanted to know why and now they did.
They knew why. But now more than ever her mind
reeled away from the truth, careened off it pinball-style.
Instead she latched onto the ancillary mysteries, the other

questions still unanswered: What had really happened to Emily Huang? Why had she left Haven? Was she really killed so she couldn't talk to Jake's dad?

Jake had gone home with a promise to call later. She was glad. She needed a break from him, from what they had learned together. He was *implicated*. She would forever associate Jake with the marshes, with the replicas, with the terrible thing growing inside of them.

Through the lit windows of the guesthouse she could see Lyra and 72 sitting together on the sofa, or at least, sitting side by side. Each of them seemed bound up in individual space, totally discrete, totally other. She wondered whether they knew she could see them, or even cared. They were likely used to being looked at. She couldn't imagine what they'd seen, and she shivered thinking about how matter-of-factly Lyra had talked about all the children in the yellow cluster dying, as if she were talking about a field being mowed or the garbage taken out for collection.

She felt trapped. She couldn't face the replicas again. But she couldn't face April either, who appeared every two minutes at the kitchen window, cupping her face to the glass to peer outside, obviously dying to peek at the replicas in the guesthouse but doing her best to respect their privacy, at Gemma's request.

Gemma knew she'd been unfair − she'd asked for help and hadn't told April anything − but the more she learned, the more impossible it was to explain. Gemma didn't want to be forced to say the words out loud. She thought the words might scorch her vocal cords, leave permanent damage, make blisters on her tongue. She wished in that moment she'd never come down to Florida, that she'd never heard of Haven at all. She imagined Whole Foods takeout and the big couch and her father safely away on the other side of the world. Kristina happy-zonked on her nighttime pills. April Snapchatting the funny-looking dogs she spotted in Florida. Even Chloe Goddamned DeWitt and her skinny-bitch wolf-pack friends. She would give anything to go back to caring about Chloe DeWitt.

But she couldn't. She sat down on a sagging lounge chair and began running a search for Emily J. Huang on her phone. It was a common name. She tried Emily J. Huang, nurse, and a result surfaced immediately: a four-year-old funeral announcement. The announcement was accompanied by a picture of a pretty Asian woman smiling into the camera. The service had been held at the First Episcopal Church in Palm Grove, Florida – she'd seen an exit sign for Palm Grove on the highway earlier.

*Emily J. Huang recently returned from a seven-year tenure with Doctors Without Borders, where she was dispatched to remote places in the world to volunteer with underserved medical communities . . .*

Emily must have made up a cover story to tell her friends and family while she was working at Haven. No wonder Nurse M's identity had never been established. Emily had been sure to keep her personal and work lives separate.

*. . . and had previously served as a staff director at a charity that placed children from high-risk backgrounds in stable environments . . .*

Gemma reread the sentence a second and then a third time. Jake had mentioned that Dr. Saperstein had founded a charity responsible for placing foster kids and orphans into homes. Could it be a coincidence? She searched Emily J. Huang and the Home Foundation and sucked in a quick breath. There were hundreds of results, many of them from newspapers or crime blogs. One of the first articles, from a Miami-based paper dated only six months before the funeral announcement, showed Emily Huang leaving a police station, her hand raised to shield her face from the cameras. Gemma took a notebook from her backpack and made notes as she was reading, hoping a pattern would emerge.

> The state attorney's office has declined to file charges against the charity the Home Foundation, after an initial inquiry showed that a number of foster children may have gone missing under its supervision. Our research puts that

number at anywhere from twenty-five to more than two hundred over a three-year period beginning in 2001, during explosive growth that eventually resulted in the Home Foundation's expansion nationwide, and consolidation into one of the most powerful and well-endowed charities in the country. Several relatives of the children who allegedly came under the Home Foundation's care have come forward to suggest that the charity be charged with abuse, neglect, and fraud. One plaintiff has even filed a suit charging the Home Foundation with abduction.

'After a careful review of the cases in question, and in consideration of the thousands of children that the Home Foundation has successfully placed and monitored in homes across the nation, we don't think there's a case here to pursue at this time,' said Assistant State Attorney Charles Lanski.

The Home Foundation has released only a single statement, in which it referred to the accusations as 'wild, bizarre, and absolutely invented.' Initially, they did not respond to a request for further statement. But later, Megan Shipman, director of publicity for the Home Foundation, followed up in an email.

'It's unfortunate that the accusations of a small group of very troubled individuals is calling into question the work of a twenty-year-old organization, which has placed more than two thousand children in safe and happy homes,' she wrote. 'Anyone who takes the accusations in context can see that they are no more than attempts to exploit human tragedy for financial gain.'

All three accusers who have come forward were, at the time of the incidents in question, heavy substance abusers. Sarah Mueller was only nineteen and a crack-cocaine addict when a woman she claims was from the Home Foundation offered her the sum of two thousand dollars for temporary custodial guardianship of her infant child, Diamond.

Speaking from the state-run rehabilitative halfway house where she currently lives, Mueller told the *Highland News*: 'I didn't think it was for good. I thought I could have her back soon as I got clean.' But when Mueller sobered up, after a long period of bouncing between the streets, jail, and rehabilitation programs, she found that the Home Foundation showed no record at all that Diamond had ever come through their system.

Mueller's story has eerie parallels to that of Fatima 'Tina' Aboud, who was barely out of her teens when a woman she describes as a Home Foundation 'nurse' came knocking. Aboud claims she was offered three thousand dollars for her son, then two years old. Aboud, who suffers from schizophrenia, agreed, believing that if she didn't, the CIA would come for her child. Ten years later, Aboud is stabilized through medication and has tried to locate her son, Benjamin, only to find the trail completely cold.

The last plaintiff to come forward is Rick Harliss, and his story is the most difficult to untangle. The *Highland News* has learned exclusively that Harliss, a sometime-handyman, was in jail after an altercation involving his then-employer, Geoffrey Ives, formerly of the pharmaceutical giant Fine & Ives.

Gemma's stomach dropped through the soles of her feet. For a second the words blurred. She blinked, trying to make them come into focus again. Still her father's name was there.

Harliss left his daughter in the care of his ex-wife, Aimee (now deceased). Aimee subsequently claimed their daughter, Brandy-Nicole, was kidnapped from the car while she was at the grocery store. But Harliss became suspicious when her account of the story changed, and when he noticed that she came into a large sum of cash at the same time Brandy-Nicole vanished.

After the *Highland News* officially broke the story of Sarah Mueller's accusations more than a year ago, Rick Harliss claims to have recognized two people from a photograph of the Home Foundation staff, including a staff nurse, Emily J. Huang, whom he claims to have seen several times with his ex-wife.

Adding to the difficulty of disentangling the truth – and fueling the idea that these claims are fraudulent – is the fact that Sarah Mueller and Fatima Aboud may have known each other previously. Both women were in a state-run rehabilitation facility during the same period of time, although counselors from the program do not recall the women being friendly. . . .

Gemma stopped reading. Her head was pounding again. She couldn't make sense of any of it. Rick Harliss had once worked for her family. Why didn't she remember him? It must have been when she was young. But how did the story of those missing children connect to Haven, to the clones, to the charity, to her father?

All she knew was that it *was* connected. Jake had originally believed Haven was doing drug experimentation on orphaned children – and he was 50 percent right. But why, if Haven was also manufacturing clones?

She did some more Googling and found out most of the alleged disappearances had occurred during the *exact same three-year period* as her father's lawsuit against his former business partner. The facts, then, were these: Dr. Saperstein got control of the institute the same year Richard Haven died and was, potentially, murdered. Around the same time, her father sued for control of the company, possibly because his business partner wanted to invest in Haven. He lost.

Meanwhile Dr. Saperstein was busy 'misplacing' children through his charity, possibly stealing them for some unimaginable purpose. Then Fine & Ives swooped in and took ownership of Haven, at least financially, and the institute began to breed clones in large quantities for its own sick purposes.

Her father had said *follow the money.* She was sure she was missing something, and she was sure it had to do with money, with the flow of cash from the military to Fine & Ives to Haven.

She Googled Rick Harliss, but although he was mentioned several times in articles related to the Home Foundation, he'd done a pretty good job of avoiding the photographers. She found a Rick Harliss who was a lawyer in Tallahassee and a Rick Harliss who had his own personal training business, but she could not find a single picture of the Rick Harliss who believed his daughter, Brandy-Nicole, had been sold to the Home Foundation. Then, remembering that he'd been in jail, she added *mug shot* to the search terms. Almost immediately, she was bounced to a website unimaginatively named Mugshot.com.

For one, two, three seconds, her heart failed to beat.

He was younger in the picture, and although his eyes

were raw-red and his expression ferocious, he was handsome. She thought of his stale, coffee-breath smell, the curtained greasiness of his hair. He had aged terribly. And yet despite the differences, there was no mistaking him.

It was the guy from the gas station. *What do you know about Haven?* And she remembered now that she had had the impression of familiarity. She'd remembered him, at least vaguely, and now she knew why. He had done work for her father. Probably he'd been one of the rotating series of guys who kept the grounds, or cleaned the pool, or painted the house.

Always she came back to her father and Haven. That was the center of the mystery, the original cancer, the tumor that had metastasized into a hundred other mysteries.

'Gemma?'

Gemma looked up. She hadn't heard April come outside. Quickly, she pocketed her phone, as if April might read it from across the pool deck.

'What are you doing out here?' April frowned, shaking her bangs from her eyes.

'Nothing. Thinking. Trying not to think.' Gemma stood up. The distance between her and April suddenly felt very great.

'You promised to explain.' April's voice was all pinched, like it had been zipped up too tightly.

Gemma rubbed her forehead. 'I know. I'm sorry. I'm still sorting it out myself.'

April came down off the porch. She was barefoot and already dressed for bed, in cotton shorts and an oversized T-shirt from Bubba Gump Shrimp Company. Gemma was struck in that moment by how normal she looked: tan, rested, beautiful. She and April had always talked about being co-aliens, members of a different species dropped on this planet to suffer among the humans, maybe pay penance for crimes committed in a past life on their home planet. But April wasn't an alien. April belonged.

And for a split second, Gemma hated her.

'Well?' April stopped a few feet away from Gemma, hugging herself. She wasn't smiling. 'I'm listening.'

Gemma looked away, ashamed. April had helped her. April was *always* helping her. But how could she begin to describe what she had seen? How could she talk about the other-Gemma, the nightmare twin? It was like something out of a horror movie.

'Haven was using the replicas,' she said, because it seemed as good a place to start as any. 'They were engineering them for a specific reason. We think Haven was infecting them with some kind of disease,' she added quickly, before she could lose her nerve.

'A disease?' April repeated. She stared openmouthed at Gemma. 'And you brought them *here*?'

'It isn't contagious like the flu is.' Gemma felt queasy thinking about it. She hoped she was right. She hadn't truly understood everything Jake was reading to her. The boy seemed all right, almost normal. But she'd seen the girl stumble. Motor coordination problems were some of the first symptoms, he had read. 'You can't get it except through tissue or organ transfers or – ingestion. And it takes years to work. It's like mad cow disease, or Alzheimer's, or something like that.'

'My grandparents would kill me,' April said, and Gemma's anger notched up again. Twenty feet away were two people who had been raised as human petri dishes, and all April could think about was getting in trouble. 'What do you think they're doing in there, anyway?'

'I don't know.' When Gemma turned, she saw they were no longer in the living room. They must be in the kitchen or bedroom, and out of view. Irrationally, she was glad. She didn't want April to see them. April didn't *deserve* to see them. 'I don't know. Eating. Sleeping. Trying to relax. Whatever people normally do.'

April laughed in a way Gemma didn't like, as if Gemma had made a joke. 'And you're sure they're not going to, like, infect us?'

'Only if you decide to go zombie on them and eat their brains,' Gemma said sarcastically, but April actually nodded, as if she was reassured. She was still staring into the guesthouse. A glass of water and an open can of Coke on the coffee table were the only signs that someone had been there at all.

'And they can, like, talk and stuff?' April asked. 'And eat normal food?'

'Yes, they can *talk and stuff.*' Gemma's voice sounded overloud, but she didn't care. 'They're *people.*' If she'd considered even for a second telling April about the girl with Gemma's face, she knew now she never would. She couldn't.

'Okay, okay. Jeez. Calm down.' April rolled her eyes, as if Gemma was the one being unreasonable. 'Sorry if I'm not a clone expert.'

'Replica,' Gemma corrected her automatically. 'They don't like being called clones.' She didn't know how she knew this, only that she'd noticed Lyra flinch whenever she used that word, the way April did when someone referred to her *dyke* parents, or Gemma did when she heard *fat.*

'Are you serious?' Again, April laughed.

'Yes, I'm serious.' She was suddenly way past anger. She was furious. She wasn't tied to the girl on the marshes and yet she was: they were bound together, they were the *same.* Which meant that Gemma had died, too. Just a little. But she had died. 'They can talk, they have feelings, they have likes and dislikes, they dream and breathe and hurt like anybody else.'

'Okay, okay. I'm sorry.' Now April was squinting at Gemma as if she didn't know her. 'I'm just a little freaked out, okay?' Gemma said nothing. 'You have to admit it's weird. . . . I mean, you said yourself they were *engineered*. Shake and bake, test-tube style.'

'I hate to remind you,' Gemma snapped, not even sure why she was so angry, 'but so were you.'

Instantly, she knew it was the wrong thing to say. April went very still. 'You're comparing me to one of *them*?' she whispered. Gemma wasn't deceived by her tone of voice. The quieter April got, the angrier she was. 'You think because my moms are gay, that makes me some kind of freak?'

Gemma already felt guilty. But it was too late to take back the words. And what would April say if she knew that Gemma had a clone floating around somewhere – possibly *more* than one? That Gemma remembered Haven from her childhood? 'I'm just saying.' She couldn't stand to see the naked hurt on April's face, so she looked away. 'Plenty of people would think you weren't in a great position to judge.'

'I know.' April's voice was sharp as a slap. 'I just didn't know you were one of them.'

She turned away and Gemma saw her bring a hand

quickly to her eyes. April *never* cried. Gemma was suddenly filled with wrenching guilt. She thought her stomach might actually twist itself up and out of her throat. She nearly put a hand on April's shoulder – she nearly begged for forgiveness – but then April spoke again.

'Maybe you should leave.' She didn't turn around, but her voice was steady and very flat, and Gemma thought maybe she'd been wrong, maybe April hadn't been crying at all.

'What?'

'You heard me. Maybe you should leave. You *and* your new best friends.' She turned just slightly, so Gemma could see the familiar ski-slope jump of her nose, the soft curve of her cheek, a sweep of dark hair, and she knew in that moment that something had changed forever. 'I'll give you until morning,' April said.

She moved soft-footed across the grass and into the house. Gemma wished she'd stomped off instead. She wished an earthquake would come, or rifts would appear in the ground – anything other than this terrible silence, the peacefulness of the crickets in the trees and the low drone of TV, the world humming along while hers was ending. April didn't once look back. After she closed the door, Gemma heard the lock turn.

Then she was alone.

# TWELVE

GEMMA WOKE FROM A NIGHTMARE with her cheek saddled up against a band of old plastic striping and the sun hard in her eyes. Immediately she remembered her fight with April. She had a horrible, sticky feeling all over, as if something wet was clinging to her. She couldn't remember her nightmare, but she was left with the disturbing idea that something had been hunting her, wouldn't leave her alone.

She sat up, touching her cheek where the chair had indented it. The windows of the main house threw back the light so she couldn't see beyond them, but she thought April must still be asleep. She checked her phone: nine thirty. She noticed her notebook wasn't on the ground where she'd left it. But she must have stuffed it into her backpack.

Even before she figured out what to do about the

replicas, she was determined to apologize to April, to *explain*. April was her best friend – her *only* good friend, unless you counted Pete, and she wasn't sure she could. April was freaked out by the replicas, but anyone would be. And Gemma had been horrible. She had deserved to sleep outside, deserved the stiffness in her neck and shoulders and the taste of dead fish in her mouth.

She would make coffee. She would apologize. She would tell April everything, including the truth about the dead girl Gemma had seen out on the marshes.

She went up the stairs and was encouraged to find the back door unlocked. It seemed like a sign that April might be ready to forgive her. The kitchen was empty, but there was coffee in the pot and a dirty plate sitting on the table next to a ketchup bottle. So April was awake. Gemma was about to call out to her when she saw the note, anchored to the counter by a red mug that said *San Francisco*.

The note was very short.

> *Going for a run and then to play tennis. Will be back around noon. Please be gone.*
> *– April*

Gemma balled it up and threw it in the trash can. She felt like throwing something but she didn't want to get in trouble with April's grandparents, so instead she opened the back door again and slammed it three times. She was furious again. Fucking April. Gemma had been out slogging through the marshes, nearly getting shot, hiding from the *military*, rooting out her family's deepest, darkest secret. *She'd found her own fucking clone.* And April had been going for a run and taking tennis lessons and was chucking Gemma out because of one stupid thing she'd said. Meanly, Gemma thought now she was even glad she'd said it.

She took a shower, leaving hair in the drain and not bothering to clean it out, and then brushed her teeth vigorously. At least she looked slightly better after sleeping, less like a zombie from a horror movie brought back to life by its taste for brains.

Downstairs, she poured some coffee into a mug – pleased, again, that she could use the last of the milk – and tried calling Jake. His phone rang but he didn't pick up. She waited a few minutes and tried again. Then, when he didn't answer, she sent him a text. *You awake?* It was only ten, but she couldn't imagine he was sleeping in, not after yesterday and all they'd discovered about Haven.

She was halfway back to the guesthouse when something crunched beneath her foot: her ChapStick, which had somehow escaped from her backpack and rolled across the pool deck. She saw now that her bag was lying on its side, and when she went to return the ChapStick to it, saw that everything inside was a jumbled mess, as if someone had rifled through it. Instinctively she reached for her wallet. Her credit cards were there, but she'd taken out three hundred dollars from the ATM in Walmart the day before, and all of it was gone.

She felt as she had the single time her mom had caved and taken Gemma to an amusement park, and they'd ridden a roller coaster called the Cobra together. As they'd inched up, up, up toward that first crest and then the first downward hurtle, Gemma had known she'd made a huge mistake, that she didn't want to see what was on the other side.

The guesthouse was empty. That was obvious as soon as she walked in. It even *felt* empty, and she was afraid to speak out loud because she didn't want to hear her voice sucked away by the carpet. Still, she went from room to room, checking the bathroom, even opening the closet doors as if Lyra and 72 might be hiding there. For a brief, delirious moment, she even imagined Lyra, 72, and April out together somewhere near the ocean, dressed in tennis whites, working on their game.

But there was no pretending. The replicas were gone.

Jake still hadn't texted her back. She tried calling again, then remembered he had said his aunt's house was pretty rural and cell phone service was bad. He'd written down his address and home phone number on the back of a piece of tinfoil that looked like it had come from a cigarette pack, and she tried calling this as well, three times in a row. She switched back to trying his cell phone, and her next two calls went straight to voice mail. She couldn't understand what it meant, but she was afraid. Printouts from the Haven Files had been recovered from the bomber's bag. It seemed obvious that he would get in trouble. Maybe he was with the cops even now. What if they thought he'd had something to do with the explosion?

It was ten thirty now, and she was getting desperate. No way was she going to be here when April returned – she'd rather hitchhike. She'd rather *walk*.

Then she remembered Pete.

He picked up on the first ring. 'This is your knight in shining armor,' he said, in a baritone. 'To whom do I have the pleasure of speaking?'

'A lady in distress,' Gemma said. The sound of his voice lifted her spirits, just a bit. 'I need help.'

Pete cleared his throat. 'You're in luck. That's what knights in shining armor *do*. Helping is basically our bread and butter. What's the trouble?'

'I need you to pick me up' – she gave him April's address in Bowling Springs – 'as soon as possible. I'll explain when you get here.'

'Aye, aye, Captain,' Pete said. 'Be there in two shakes of a lamb's tail.'

'What does that even mean?'

'It means sit tight. I'm coming.'

She hung up, feeling better already. Pete could be annoying, but he was reliable and sweet. A distraction, too. Kind of like having a fluffy Pomeranian for company. If Pomeranians could drive and knew all the words to 'Baby Got Back.'

He was there in less than half an hour, and her heart lifted again when she saw the ridiculous purple minivan swanning down the road. He leaned over to pop open the door for her, and she nearly sat on a bag of doughnuts in the passenger seat.

'Figured you hadn't eaten,' he said. 'There's coffee, too, if you want it.' Two jumbo Styrofoam cups were straining against the cup holders.

Pete must have gotten sun yesterday, because his arms and the bridge of his nose were more deeply freckled. But the freckles looked good on him, like a dusting of stars. She was super aware of the fact that when she sat, her shorts cut hard into her thighs, and wished she had worn jeans instead. Even her *knees* looked fat. To conceal her embarrassment she looked down, fumbling with the lid of her coffee.

'You weren't kidding about the knight-in-shining-armor thing,' she said.

He beamed at her. Actually beamed. His smile nearly blinded her. 'So where to?'

She knew that there was no point in trying to go after the replicas. She wasn't Sherlock Holmes, and there were no footprints to track. They had most likely left in the middle of the night and could have been anywhere. She needed to talk to Jake. He might have ideas about what to do next. Fortunately, he'd written down his address when he'd given her his aunt's landline. At least the replicas hadn't stolen her entire wallet. Small mercies.

'Here.' She fished out the piece of foil and handed it over to Pete. He raised his eyebrows.

'Is this a clue or something?' Pete said. 'Because I think it was Sergeant Pepper in the pantry with an egg cozy.'

'Just drive, okay? I need to talk to my friend Jake,' she said. 'He's not picking up his phone.'

Instantly, Pete's face changed. 'When you said *help*, I didn't think you needed a ride to your boyfriend's,' he said, and although he put the car in drive, she could tell he was hurt.

'Jake isn't my boyfriend. Trust me,' she said. 'He's –' She was about to say he was way out of her league, but she didn't think this would make Pete feel any better. Especially since she was kind of starting to hope Pete might be *in* her league. 'Look, he's been helping me. It's complicated. . . .' She trailed off.

Pete made a face, as if he wasn't convinced. 'So why couldn't Prince Charming come and get you?'

'I told you. I can't get in touch with him,' Gemma said, and Pete snorted. 'Look, you've got it wrong. Jake's dad was a big Haven freak. After he died, Jake kind of took over for him.'

'Haven?' Pete looked confused. 'The place we heard about on the radio? The one that got blown up?'

'Yeah. That one.' Gemma took a deep breath. The GPS was directing them out of the subdivision now, speaking in its measured mechanical voice, and Gemma found herself unconsciously scanning the streets for April in her jogging clothes. She was seized by the sudden idea that once they turned onto the highway, that was it. She would never see April again. And she knew, in part, it had been her fault. She should have talked to April, trusted her sooner, let her in on the secret, explained. She turned back to Pete. 'There's a lot of stuff I haven't told you. It's going to sound crazy, okay? If I tell you, you're going to think I'm bananas. You have to promise not to think that.'

'I swear,' Pete said. He didn't seem upset anymore.

'*Turn right on County Route 39,*' said the voice of the GPS. Gemma looked once more for April, and the streets were totally empty. As if they were just waiting for something, or someone.

'It's kind of a long story,' Gemma said. Her heart was elbowing up against her rib cage, like it was trying to force its way through them. How would she even begin?

Pete smiled, just a little. 'You've got eighty-seven miles,' he said, reaching for the doughnuts. 'So start talking.'

It was easy to talk to Pete. Gemma hadn't expected him to be such a good listener, but he was. He didn't interrupt with stupid questions or squawk in disbelief when she told him about stumbling across the replicas – *literally* stumbling – in the marshes. Only once did he interrupt, when she described finding the dead girl with her exact face. Her replica. And then he just said, 'Jesus,' and then, 'Go on.'

By the time she finished telling him everything – about the long slog back through the marshes, and the folder that Lyra had smuggled out of Haven, about *transmissible spongiform encephalopathies*; about waking up to discover the replicas missing with all her money; about Jake and his dad and the Haven Files and Angel Fire and her mission from God – they had reached Jake's road.

Jake hadn't been lying about his aunt's house being rural. Route 12, on the outskirts of Little Waller, was a treacherous narrow dirt path studded with holes. On either side of the road, behind growth so riotous it looked like the trees were launching some kind of major offensive, prefab houses, little more than glorified trailers, sagged in the midday sun, doing their best to stay on their feet in the wilting heat. Gemma felt an unexpected rise of pity. No wonder Jake had been obsessing about his father's death for years. She couldn't imagine there was much else to do. This was a lonely place.

They had to squeeze by a Florida Energy truck that was teetering in a deep gutter on one side of the lane; a man in a hard hat was high on the pole, fiddling with the wire, and a group of workers were doing nothing but watching. Gemma was relieved to see that Jake's car was in the driveway, or the small patch of dirt that counted as one. For the first time she noticed the bumper was plastered with bumper stickers, so overlayered and old that most were illegible. She wondered whether it had been his father's car.

Pete pulled into the driveway behind Jake's car but made no move to get out. Instead he hunched forward over the steering wheel, peering up at the house. It was an ugly yellow color, with brown shutters, two of which were hanging at weird angles. Someone had made an effort to clear a patch of front lawn – Gemma thought of Jake, lining up his utensils neatly, and imagined it must be him – but the trees were reclaiming their territory slowly and the window boxes were empty except for dirt. No one had taken much pride in the house, for sure.

'Well,' Pete said, with his usual cheerfulness. 'At least we won't have to take our shoes off.'

Gemma licked her lips. The coffee had been too sugary and now her mouth had a weird, gritty feel. Pete still hadn't responded to her story, not directly. Maybe he didn't believe her. 'Look. All the stuff I told you . . .'

Pete turned to her. His eyes were the color of Rufus's. Toffee brown, warm. 'You can trust me,' he said. It was as though he read her mind. 'I won't tell anyone.'

It was as if a bubble of air in her chest had been released. 'So . . . you don't think I'm crazy?'

'People who pay five bucks for coffee are crazy,' he said. Then he frowned. 'But you're in some deep shit.' She'd never heard him sound so serious, and in that moment she realized he was handsome. Not just cute. Not goofy-looking. *Handsome.* Clean jaw and a little bit of stubble, all those golden freckles, the hair falling softly across his forehead. 'I'm worried about you. Powerful people went to a lot of trouble to keep Haven's work a secret. My guess is they won't stop now.'

'No one knows we were out on the marshes,' Gemma said. Her stomach squirmed, though. 'No one knows what we found.'

'So you think,' Pete said. And then, in a quieter voice,

'I'm not trying to scare you. But we have to be careful.'
It was amazing, Gemma thought, how nice the word *we*
could sound, and she nearly put her arms around him. She
nearly kissed him.

Christ. She was fantasizing about kissing Pervy Pete.
April would never believe it. *If* April ever spoke to her
again.

It was hotter here than it had been in April's grandparents' subdivision, despite all the shade. Gemma felt sorry
for the Florida Energy guys.

'You'll like Jake,' Gemma said, partly to convince herself. The tree branches lifted and fell silently, touched by a
phantom wind. She didn't know why she felt so nervous.
Something about the whole place was creepy, like the set
piece of an abandoned road from a horror film after the
zombie apocalypse has struck.

Pete shrugged. But he still looked unhappy, or nervous, or both. 'Weird are my people,' he said. 'Weird is
what I do.'

'He'll have a plan. You'll see,' she said, partly to reassure herself. A tabby cat was sunning itself on the grungy
porch and stared insolently at them as the sound of the
doorbell echoed through the house. *You shouldn't be here,*
it seemed to be saying, and Gemma couldn't help but feel
the same way.

For a long minute, she heard no sounds of movement.

She began to feel not just nervous but truly afraid. She jabbed a finger on the bell again and at the same time tried the knob. Locked. Finally she heard footsteps. In the window next to the door, she saw Jake twitch open the blinds, and his dark eyes peer between them. Then the sound of the lock releasing. Relief felt like something physical, like something she could lie down in.

'God,' she said, when he opened the door. 'I was afraid something had happened. I was afraid . . .' But she trailed off, seeing that he had only opened the door a crack and he was angling his body so they couldn't come inside.

'What are you doing here?' He was looking at her as if he'd never seen her before in his life. He looked *furious*.

It wasn't exactly the welcome she'd been expecting. Next to her, Pete pivoted, staring back toward the street as though considering a quick getaway.

'You weren't picking up your phone,' Gemma said. 'I called a dozen times.'

'Can't find my phone,' he said. 'Don't know what happened to it.' His eyes swept the street behind them. 'You should really go.' He started to close the door.

'Wait.' Gemma got a hand in the door. For a second he looked like he was considering closing it on her fingers, but then he thought better of it. 'You don't understand. The replicas – they're gone.'

'Quiet.' Jake hushed her as though she'd cursed in church. She was close enough to see that he was sweating. Fear. Jake Witz, she realized, wasn't angry. He was terrified. 'Keep your voice down.'

'We came here for your help —' Pete started to say, but Gemma cut him off. She felt wild and reckless and dizzyingly confused.

'Didn't you hear me? They're *gone*,' she said. 'They must have left in the middle of the night. They took my money. Maybe they took your phone, too —'

'I heard you.' Once again, Jake's eyes went to the street. 'It's not my problem. Not yours, either. Now get out of here. You shouldn't have come. I don't know you, okay?' He raised his voice. He was practically shouting. 'I don't even know you.'

Once again Gemma stopped Jake from closing the door, just barely, on her fingers. She kept her hand in the doorjamb so he couldn't. She had that hard-throat feeling of trying not to cry. 'What happened?' she said. 'Are you in trouble with the cops?'

'The cops.' Jake let out a sound that could have been a laugh or a cough. 'Not the cops.' He took a step forward, startling Gemma and forcing her to release the doorjamb. 'My lights are working just fine,' he added almost angrily, leaning so close that Gemma could feel his breath on her face. Before she could ask him what he meant, he closed the door, and the lock slid back into place.

For a second Gemma just stood there, stunned. Even with Pete standing next to her, she had never felt so alone in her life. She was too embarrassed to look at Pete. She'd dragged him all the way here, promising that Jake would help, and he hadn't even let them inside. 'Something must have happened. He wasn't like this yesterday.' She thought of the way he'd looked, with sweat standing on his skin, and what he'd said to her: *My lights are working just fine.*

'Gemma.' There was a warning in Pete's voice, but she was too upset to listen to it.

'Someone must have gotten to him – yesterday he was practically *begging* me for information –'

'*Gemma.*' This time, Pete seized her hand, and she was surprised into silence by the sudden contact. Her palms were sweaty, but his were dry and cool and large. 'Funny they need so many guys to work the wires, don't you think?' he said in a low voice, as he piloted her off the porch and back toward the van. He didn't look at the Florida Energy men a little ways down the road, but she could tell by the way he was staring straight ahead that he was *trying* not to look.

Instinctively, she glanced over to where the six or seven workers in their hard hats and vests were still standing – *doing nothing* – and had the sense that they had only avoided meeting her eyes by a fraction of a second. And then she understood what Jake had said about the lights.

Not nonsense. A code. *My lights are working just fine.* Meaning: no reason for the Florida Energy truck, and the people gathered across the street with their van spiky with antennae. Although Gemma had looked away as quickly as possible, she had caught the eye of one of the men down the road: clean-shaven, hard-eyed, pale as paper. Not the complexion of someone who spent every day working outside.

Jake was being watched. Which meant: they were now being watched, too. No wonder Jake had practically shoved them off his doorstep, had shouted that he didn't know them. He'd been trying to protect them. She had the overwhelming urge to turn around, to hurtle back up to the door and pound to be let in and to thank him. But that would be beyond stupid. Instead she walked stiff-backed to the minivan and climbed in, trying to appear unconcerned, as if maybe the whole thing really had been a mistake. Maybe the men – whoever they were – would believe that they were just casual acquaintances of Jake's, there to return something or say hello.

In the car, Pete wiped his hands on his jeans before grabbing hold of the steering wheel. They didn't speak. Pete kept glancing in the rearview mirror as he backed out of the driveway. *Please don't follow us,* Gemma thought.

She pressed the desire through her fists. *Don't follow us.*
But a moment later, a maroon Volvo pulled out of another
hard-packed dirt driveway and crept up behind them.
Could it be a coincidence? She didn't think so.

'Do you think – ?' she started to ask, but Pete cut her
off.

'Not now,' he said. 'Need to think.' Somehow, the
fact that Pete – Pete of the endless, stream-of-consciousness
babble – had run out of things to say scared her even more
than the car behind them.

It wasn't a coincidence: the car followed them no
matter how many turns they made down shitty country
roads, even after they reached downtown Little Waller,
such as it was: a few bleak roads studded with tire shops,
fast-food restaurants, and liquor and discount stores. The
driver didn't even bother going for subtlety – and this,
too, scared Gemma, and made her angry. It was the way
a cat toyed with its prey, batting it around a bit, taking its
time, certain already of its satisfaction.

'We need to lose them.' Gemma hardly recognized her
voice when she spoke. It was as if an alien had crawled
into her throat and taken over her vocal cords.

'*Lose* them?' Pete repeated. Gemma realized how
tense Pete was. He was practically doubled over the
steering wheel, staring hard at the road as if it might
simply disappear. 'Christ. You're really taking the

knight-in-shining-armor thing to the limit, you know that?' He yanked the wheel hard to the left, and Gemma was thrown against the door. But only thirty seconds later, lazily, the Volvo turned, too. It was so absurd that they were riding around in an eggplant-colored minivan. They might as well be driving a hovercraft. It wasn't exactly like they could *blend*. 'Who are these guys, anyway?'

'Maybe cops,' Gemma said. She had an awful, heavy feeling in her gut, like she was trying to digest a roll of toilet paper. She'd dragged Pete into this. She'd dragged them *all* into this. 'Probably military.'

'Military.' Pete repeated the word as if he'd never heard it before. His freckles were standing out ever more clearly from his skin, like even they were thinking of making a break for it. 'Jesus . . .'

'You told me you wanted to help.' Gemma was squeezing her hands so tightly she was sure she'd break the skin.

Pete sighed. 'I do,' he said. 'I just didn't think we'd end up in a chase scene so early in the movie.' Then: 'All right, look. Are you buckled in?'

Gemma nodded. She was too nervous to speak. A sign ahead pointed the way to the interstate, and here there were more cars on the road, funneling onto or off the highway. The Volvo was still following them, but at a distance of about fifty yards.

Pete put on his blinker and moved into the far left lane, as though he was about to turn across traffic and into a shopping mall that boasted two liquor stores, a nail salon, and a pizza joint. At least one car crowded in behind them, separating them temporarily from the Volvo's view. The traffic light turned red. Pete inched forward. Gemma could hear him breathing. She felt as if she *couldn't* breathe, as if she was being squeezed between two iron plates.

'What are you . . . ?' she started to say, but then the light turned green and Pete slammed his foot on the accelerator.

The engine whined, then yanked them forward. Gemma nearly cracked her head on the dashboard before she was pulled backward by the seat belt, smacking her head against the seat. Pete jerked the wheel to the right, cutting across two lanes of traffic. Several drivers leaned a long protest on their horns, and a Chevy screeched to a stop to avoid colliding with them.

'What the hell? What the hell?' Gemma was screaming, and more horns went off as Pete careened onto the entrance to the interstate. But then it was over. He was speeding up the on ramp. Traffic blurred past them, a solid moving mass of cars dazzled by sunlight, and then they were there, passing among them, and the Volvo was long gone. The sky was bright and puffy with clouds.

They could have been anyone, going anywhere.

'How's that for a chase scene?' Pete said. He was out of breath.

Gemma couldn't help it: all her fear transformed into the sudden desire to laugh. It practically lifted her out of her seat. She doubled forward, holding her stomach, laughing so hard it hurt. Pete started to laugh, too. Then he snorted, which just made Gemma laugh harder, until she couldn't breathe and had to lean back, gasping.

'Not bad,' she said. Her eyes were watering, blurring her vision of the highway and the featureless towns on either side of it, all of them identical, replicas of one another. 'Not bad at all.'

# THIRTEEN

THEY DROVE FOR ANOTHER HOUR. Pete switched onto different freeways several times, just in case, although Gemma couldn't imagine how anyone could still be pursuing them. She was surprised to see a sign for Palm Grove – the town where Emily Huang, the nurse at Haven who'd been killed before she could talk to Mr. Witz, had lived – and equally surprised when Pete turned off the highway.

'What are you doing?' she asked.

'I'm starving,' he said. 'I'm seriously about to self-cannibalize. And I need both hands to drive.'

'I'm hungry too,' Gemma said, before remembering that she tried never to admit to being hungry in front of other people. But of course, the fact that they'd just escaped from a military tail made her normal concerns about being overweight seem unimportant. Besides, Pete didn't look at her that way, as if there was something wrong with her, as if she *really shouldn't*, as if she would *be pretty if only she'd slim down a bit*.

She liked how Pete looked at her.

They pulled over at a diner across from a motel called the Starlite, its parking lot empty except for a white Chevrolet and a few beat-up, dusty sedans. She didn't want to think about the kind of people who used the Starlite midday. Gemma climbed out, stretching, her body still sore from being contorted on a lawn chair all night. Once again she had that awful, full-body sensation of being watched. She whipped around, certain she saw a face peering out at her from a window of the Starlite. But it was only a trick of the light.

Still, even after they were seated and tucking into enormous burgers and a platter of fries so towering it seemed to defy physics, she kept glancing out the window. Another car pulled into the diner parking lot and her heart stopped. But it was only a dad and his two kids. And after a while, she began to relax.

'So what's the next move?' Pete had waited until they were both finished eating before leaning forward and speaking to her in a low voice. 'I mean, we can't depend on Jake anymore. The replicas are gone. Are we finished here?'

Again, she liked his use of the word *we*. 'I've been

thinking about that.' She'd eaten too much too quickly and now she was nauseous. 'I have to talk to my parents. It's the only way.' Even saying it made her chest feel like it might collapse, but she kept talking, half hoping to convince herself. 'My dad has answers. He's been miserable for years, and I think it *has* to be because of Haven.' She was surprised to realize, as soon as she said it, that this was true. 'He walks around like he's got something clinging to his back. Like a giant vampire bat or something.'

Pete made a face.

'What?' she said. 'You think that's a bad idea?'

'I think it's a *great* idea.' Pete sighed. He swiped a hand through his hair. It stood up again immediately. 'This is big stuff. These are big, serious people. I worry . . .' He looked up at her, and something in his eyes made her breath snag. But he quickly looked away. 'I was worried, that's all.' He was back to his normal self, easy and silly. 'You ready to hit the road, then? I made a playlist for the drive back, you know. "One hundred greatest bluegrass hits of the 1970s."'

'I'll throw you through the windshield,' Gemma said. She felt surprisingly free now that she'd made the decision — as if something had clambered off *her* back. 'Meet me in the car, okay?'

In the bathroom she stood in front of the mirror and remembered the girl on the marshes, her reflection, her other. She leaned over the sink and splashed water on her face, as though it would help wash the image from her head. The cold did her good.

She was going to confront her father and get answers, and she didn't care anymore whether he got angry, whether he ever spoke to her again, whether he ordered her out of the house.

She almost hoped he would.

She would be fine on her own. She was stronger than she'd ever thought she was. She was strong, period.

Outside, she saw Pete sitting very still with both hands on the wheel, staring at her with the strangest expression. He must be far more freaked out than he was letting on. His eyes looked enormous, like they might simply roll out of his head, and she felt a burst of gratitude for him. He was trying, for her sake, to act normal.

'All right, Rogers.' She was speaking even as she yanked open the door. 'Passenger gets DJ privileges, so hands off the radio –' All her breath left her body at once.

There was a man sitting directly behind Pete, holding a gun to his head. She knew him instantly: it was the man who'd grabbed her outside the gas station. The same long, greasy hair, the same gray stubble and wild look.

'Get in the car and shut the door,' he said. His eyes went left, right, left, right. She wanted to move, but she was frozen. Even the air had turned leaden. She was drowning where she stood. 'In the car,' he said again, practically spitting. She saw the gun trembling in his hand and realized he was panicking. She nearly tripped getting into the car. She felt as if her whole body was coming apart.

'Okay,' she managed to say. She got the door shut and held up both hands. *Think, think.* Her phone was in her pocket. If she could somehow dial 9-1-1 . . . 'Okay, listen. Just calm down, okay? Let's everyone stay calm. You can have my wallet. You can have anything you want.'

'I didn't come for money,' the man said. He nudged Pete with the gun. Pete had gone so pale Gemma could see a vein, blue and fragile-looking, stretching across his temple. 'Drive.' She was amazed that Pete managed to get out of the parking lot without hitting anything. She was amazed by Pete, period. She'd never been so scared in her life. Her stomach was cramping, and she was worried she might go to the bathroom right there.

'Please,' she said. Her voice came out in a whisper. 'Please. What do you want?'

'I'm not going to hurt you,' he said. But he didn't sound as if he meant it. Gemma could smell him sweating in his old camouflage jacket. *Rick Harliss.* The name came back to her from the article she had read about Emily Huang and her involvement with the Home Foundation. He'd once worked for her father. He'd lost a daughter,

Brandy-Nicole, when he went to jail. 'I just want to talk, okay? That's all I want. That's all I ever wanted. Someone to listen. No one fucking listens, no one believes. . . .'

He was getting agitated. His hand was shaking again. She was worried he might accidentally discharge the gun.

'We'll listen,' she said. 'We'll listen all you want. Isn't that right, Pete?'

'Sure,' he said. His voice cracked. He licked his lips. 'Of course we will.'

'Keep going,' Rick Harliss said, giving Pete a nudge in the neck again when he started to slow down at a yellow light. Instead Pete sped through it. 'Highway,' Harliss said, when they came up on signs for I-27, and a sour taste flooded Gemma's mouth. Somehow getting on the highway made everything seem irreversible. Not like she would have rolled out of the car at a red light, but still.

She closed her eyes. She needed to focus. 'Okay, you want to talk. So let's talk, okay?' She'd heard once that in abduction situations it was important to share personal information, to get chatty, to humanize yourself. 'Let's start with names, okay? This is my friend Pete. Pete has terrible taste in music –'

'Shut up,' Harliss said. 'I'm trying to think.'

'– but he's a decent guy, all around, really. Probably the most decent guy I've ever met.' Gemma realized, even as she said it, how true it was. Poor Pete and the mess she'd dragged him into. And he'd never complained, not once. If they made it through without getting shot or butchered, she was going to buy him a lifetime supply of gummy bears.

She was going to kiss him.

'Gemma,' Pete said softly, and his voice held a warning, but she didn't care.

'And my name is Gemma Ives,' she said. 'Germ Ives. At least that's what the girls in my grade always called me, because I was sick a lot as a kid –'

'I know who you are.' Harliss's voice cracked. 'Jesus. Stop talking, okay? You're making my head hurt.'

Gemma pressed her hands hard into her thighs, digging with her fingernails, letting the pain focus her. She was scared to anger him further. But she had to make him see that she understood, that she knew him. That she was on his side. She had to buy them time. 'I know who you are, too, Mr. Harliss.'

Pete sucked in a sharp breath. For a split second the silence in the car was electric, and she worried she'd made a mistake. She was in too deep to stop now. She had to keep talking.

'You used to work for my dad, didn't you? I must have been just a little kid. But still. That day at the gas station. My dog recognized you. After all these years, he knew your smell.'

'What did your dad tell you about me?' Harliss asked. He sounded like he was talking through a mouth full of nails.

'He didn't tell me anything,' Gemma said. She didn't dare risk turning around. 'I read about you. I read about you and about your girl – Brandy-Nicole. She disappeared when she was just a baby.' Harliss whimpered. 'I know you think that the Home Foundation had something to do with it. But I'm telling you, Pete and I don't know anything. We're just as confused as you are –'

'Bullshit.' The word was an explosion. Pete winced and Gemma bit her lip, trying not to cry. 'Your dad was in it up to his neck. Don't tell me you don't know. It was all because of Haven. It was his fault they needed money. It was his fault they started grabbing kids in the first place. Your dad knew. He fucking knew all about it.' Rick Harliss took the gun from Pete's head for just a second, just long enough to wipe his nose on his sleeve. Before Gemma could do anything, or even contemplate doing anything, it was back. 'They took her from me.'

'Please,' Gemma said. 'We can help you. We'll get people to listen to you. But please just let us go. . . .'

He shook his head. 'I'm sorry,' he said. He did sound sorry. They were coming up on an exit for Randolph. He gestured to it with the gun. 'Pull off here. This is far enough.'

He directed them to a Super 8 motel. They climbed out of the car. Gemma first, carefully, conscious of the gun angling in her direction as if it were a live thing, a dog snapping at its tether, trying to get loose. Pete and Rick Harliss left the car together. Rick kept his gun, now concealed inside his sweatshirt pocket, trained on Pete's back. He herded Pete and Gemma together, forcing them to walk side by side directly in front of him, so they shuffled awkwardly toward the lobby together, bumping elbows. Rick Harliss kept stepping on Gemma's heel. It would have been funny if it weren't so awful.

'Some knight I am,' Pete said quietly. He found Gemma's hand and squeezed. When he tried to let go, she interlaced their fingers instead. 'I'm sorry, Gemma.'

She almost couldn't speak. '*You're* sorry?' She shook her head. 'This is all *my* fault.'

'Quiet,' Harliss said as they jostled together through the door. Gemma felt like a Ping-Pong ball bouncing around a tiny space. She was sure the receptionist would notice something was wrong – she was desperately hoping for it – and kept trying to telegraph desperation through her eyes. *He's got a gun. He's got a gun.*

But the receptionist was flipping through a magazine and barely even glanced up at them.

'Can I help you?' She had long pink nails with faded

decals on them. Sunflowers.

'We need a room.' Harliss pulled out some crumpled twenties and placed them on the counter.

'One or two?'

'Just one.'

The receptionist briefly lifted her eyes but they only went to the money before dropping back to the magazine, seemingly exhausted. 'Room's forty-five a night.'

'It says forty out front.'

'Rates went up.'

'Don't you think you should change the sign, then?'

There was a plastic fern in the corner, cheap blue wall-to-wall carpeting on the floor, a gun at their backs. Gemma felt the same way she did when she was dreaming – so much was true and familiar and then there was always some weird element distorted or inserted, a talking bird, the ability to fly. Finally Harliss forked over another five-dollar bill – Gemma caught herself nearly offering to pay before remembering that Harliss was kidnapping them – and they went bumping and jostling again back into the sunshine. Room 33 was on the second floor, up a narrow flight of cement stairs covered in graffiti, at the far end of the open-air corridor. Not that they could have shouted or banged on a wall, anyway. They appeared to be the only guests at the Super 8.

The room reeked of stale cigarettes. Once they were

inside, Rick Harliss bolted and chain-locked the door and drew the blinds. For several long seconds, it was dark enough that Gemma saw bursts of color and patterns blooming in the blackness of her vision. Then Harliss turned on the lamp, its shade yellowed and torn. He sat down on the bed. He removed his gun from his pocket and Gemma drew in a breath. But to her surprise he placed it in the bedside table, on top of the Bible, and closed the drawer.

'I told you,' he said. 'I don't want to hurt you. Sit.' He gestured to the second twin bed. 'Come on, sit,' he said again, raking his fingers through his thinning hair, so it stood up. Gemma remembered that he'd been handsome at one point. Strange that time could do that to a person, just work like a hacksaw on them.

Gemma and Pete moved to the bed together, as if they were tethered by an invisible cord. Once they were sitting, they were separated from Harliss by only a few feet of space, and Gemma noticed the cheapness of his jacket and oiliness of his skin and the way his fingernails were picked raw, and found herself feeling not scared of him anymore but just *sorry* for him. She realized in that second she actually believed he didn't want to hurt them. She was sure he wouldn't even be able to if he tried.

'I told you,' she said, speaking gently, as if he were a child. 'We know even less than you do. That's why I came down here. Because I *didn't* know anything. Because I was in the dark about Haven.'

'Huh. That's funny.' Harliss laughed without smiling. 'I'd think you'd have wanted to know all about it.'

Gemma's hairs stood up. She felt in the room a subtle shift – an electric stillness. 'What do you mean?'

Harliss looked up at her with those sad-dog eyes. 'Well, that's where they made you, isn't it?'

# FOURTEEN

SHE WAS DIMLY AWARE THAT Harliss was still talking. She felt as if a hole had opened inside of her and she was dropping into it.

*Made there.* She'd been made there.

Just like that girl on the marshes . . .

Gemma wasn't the original. She, too, was a replica.

*Impossible,* she wanted to say. She remembered all those baby pictures with her mom in the hospital. Could they have been staged? No. No one could fake her mother's look of exultation and exhaustion, the sweat standing out on her forehead, the look of bewildered joy. *Impossible.* But she couldn't make her voice work, and it was Pete who said it.

'That's impossible,' Pete said. He was staring at her and she turned away, too numb even to be embarrassed. He sounded horrified. Why wouldn't he be?

'. . . took me a long time to put it together,' Harliss was saying. 'I had nothing else to do, sitting there in state for twelve years. Not saying I didn't deserve it. I did. I used to do work around your house, you know, before they brought you back from that place. But I was all banged up. Got hooked on the shit they gave me for my back. I was out of my mind half the time.'

'You're out of your mind now,' Pete said. 'It's *not possible.*'

If Harliss heard Pete, he gave no sign of it. He was still looking directly at Gemma. 'My ex-lady used to do some cleaning. Your mom was in real bad shape then. Real bad. She'd just lost her baby. SIDS. That's sudden infant death syndrome, you know. Poor thing was only six months old.'

Gemma's heart stopped. 'What baby?' she managed to whisper. She'd never heard her parents mention another baby.

But Harliss just barreled on. 'Aimee — that's my ex — used to say it was funny, all the money in the world but still you can't buy your way out of that. When Aimee got pregnant with Brandy-Nicole, your mom would just sit there with her hand on Aimee's belly, trying to feel the baby kick. She started cutting out articles, you know, how Aimee should be eating, how she was supposed to be laying off booze and cigarettes. Even bought us some stuff, a crib and a stroller, some baby clothes. You could tell she was all broken up. Your mom said she couldn't get pregnant again. Something about what had happened when the first was coming out.'

There had been another one, a sister, a baby Gemma had never known about. Kristina had lost a baby. And somewhere deep in Gemma's mind an idea was growing, thoughts like storm clouds knitting together before they burst.

'When Brandy-Nicole was ten months old, I got picked up for holding and was sent to Johnston for eighteen months. That's a state prison near Smithfield. Reduced to twelve for good behavior. The day I was out I started using again.' He touched his neck once, briefly, as if amazed to find a pulse still there, to find himself alive. 'Your dad was decent. He knew I'd been sent away but he gave me the job back. I told him I was cleaned up. He believed me.'

*Life doesn't hand out second chances.* Wasn't that what her father was always saying? But at some point he'd thought differently.

There was another baby. . . .

'Well, Aimee was still going over sometimes to clean. You were home by then, and only six months younger than our Brandy-Nicole. But your mom didn't like you two to play together. She hardly let anyone near you. We thought it was because she was worried you'd get sick like the first one.'

The first one. The first daughter. The original. And she, Gemma: a shade.

'Funny, though, Aimee said to me. They look just the same. Could have been twins, she said, except for Emma had a birthmark on her arm. I didn't think much of it at the time. Only later, when I started figuring what Haven was for and what your dad had paid them for, I put two and two together.'

Emma. She had a name, this phantom sister who was so much more than that. Gemma closed her eyes and thought of her mother, sweaty and exhausted and triumphant, a baby nestled in her arms. Not Gemma. *Emma.*

All these years, Kristina had lived with a reminder of that first, lost daughter. Emma. What a pretty name; much prettier than Gemma. She was the original. Gemma was the copy. And everyone knew copies were never as good. Was that why her mom had started taking so many pills? Oxycontin and Pristiq and Klonopin and Zoloft? An A–Z array of pharmaceuticals, all so that she could forget and deny.

All because Gemma was a monster.

'The Frankenstein mask.' She opened her eyes. 'You threw the Halloween mask.' She remembered what her father had said about Frankenstein: *In the original story, in the real version, he's the one who made the monster.* She'd thought he meant it because she was awkward, and sick, and fat. But he'd meant it literally. Truthfully.

Harliss tugged at his shirt collar, and she saw a small cross tattooed on the left side of his neck. 'I was mad,' he said. 'I tried to talk to your dad. Went to his office. He said he'd call the cops on me if I came around again. Said I was harassing him. But you've got to understand. I just want answers. I need to know.'

Pete stood up, cursing. 'This is crazy,' he said. He moved toward the door, and Harliss didn't try and stop him. Gemma thought he might try to leave, but instead he just stood there. 'This is crazy, you know that?'

Gemma didn't bother responding. It wasn't crazy. In fact, for the first time, everything made sense. The fact that her father could hardly stand to look at her. The strange tension between her parents, as if they existed on either side of a chasm, a secret that had fissured their world in two. Gemma's memory of the statue and all those early hospital visits – she was probably fragile because she'd been *engineered*. She wondered if this was God's way of getting vengeance on the people who'd been made so unnaturally. He was always trying to *un*make them.

'What happened to your daughter?' she said. Her voice didn't sound like her own. 'What happened to Brandy-Nicole?'

Harliss clasped his hands. He might have been praying, except for the whiteness of his knuckles. Gemma knew he must be squeezing so hard it hurt. 'It was pretty bad in those days,' he said quietly. 'Me and Aimee was always at each other's throats. Money, mostly. We never had any. We burned through it. We were both getting high every night. Poor Brandy-Nicole wasn't even three yet. . . .' His voice broke. 'One time I woke up and she'd wet herself, made a mess all over in the middle of the night. Had to lie in it for hours. I was passed out cold all night, and Aimee hadn't even bothered coming home. That's when we split up for good.'

Shockingly, Gemma had the urge to comfort him, to tell him it was all right. But of course it wasn't.

'I needed money bad.' His voice was barely a whisper. She wondered whether he had ever told this story before. At the door, Pete was still standing there. Frozen. Horrified. 'I was still doing work for your dad. All that money everywhere . . .' His eyes slid away from Gemma's. Guilty. 'At first I just pocketed a few things. Stuff no one would notice. Pawned it off direct. I know it was wrong, but you got to understand. I wasn't thinking straight –'

Gemma shook her head to say, *It doesn't matter.*

Harliss licked his lips. 'But then I started thinking about a bigger payday. You know, something hefty. I thought your dad must have something he didn't want other people to know — there's always dirt, especially for guys like him —' Again his eyes skated nervously to Gemma's, but she didn't correct him. She wouldn't defend her father ever again.

'You're talking blackmail,' Pete said. His voice sounded very loud.

Harliss nodded. 'That was the idea, yeah.' He looked like he was about to apologize again. Gemma cut him off.

'What happened?'

He took a deep breath. 'I went digging around your dad's office, through his emails.' He squirmed. 'Like I said, I was out of my mind —'

'Go on,' Gemma said. She felt weirdly breathless, as if a giant hand were squeezing her lungs.

'I couldn't figure a way into his work files. Too much security. But I was looking for dirt closer to home, anyway. I got into his personal account. *Trouble*. That was the subject header of one of the very first emails. *Trouble*.'

The air in the motel was very still. Gemma had the sense that even the dust motes were hanging motionless in the air, suspended and breathless.

'I didn't understand any of it. Not then. It was all about some kind of investment your father had made. Your dad was pulling out. Said he'd given plenty of money already and wanted nothing to do with it anymore, said he'd figured out it was wrong. And this man, Mark Saperstein, wanted more money out of him. He said with Haven going in a new direction, it was going to make them all rich in the end if only your dad would get Fine and Ives on board. I remember one phrase exact: *They die early anyway.* That was at the end of Saperstein's message.'

Gemma felt the space between her heartbeats as long moments of blank nonexistence. What had they learned in biology about clones? Imperfect science. Cancers, tumors that grew like flower buds in manufactured lungs and hearts and livers. It was as if the growth of their cells, unnaturally jump-started, couldn't afterward be stopped.

She wondered how old she would be when her cells began to double and triple and worse.

'Your dad caught me. Not then, but another time, in his office. High as a kite. He was pissed. After all he'd done for me, giving me another chance. Don't blame him. Cops found some of your parents' stuff back at our place, too. A watch and other stuff. I'd been too fucked up to offload it all. Getting careless. They booked me for theft and possession, too, since they found a few bags around my place. This time I got sent away for longer, because it wasn't the first time. But first I spent a couple of weeks in a detox unit.

'Detox nearly killed me. I was so sick. I prayed that I would die. But I didn't.' His hand moved again to the cross on his neck. 'Afterward I swore I'd never touch none of that shit again. And I haven't. That was fourteen years ago. I haven't even taken a sip of beer and I won't, never again.' Those eyes, surprisingly warm, surprisingly attractive, buried in that damaged face: Gemma could hardly stand to look at him. 'It's my fault Brandy-Nicole got taken. If I hadn't been high, if I hadn't got sent away, she'd still be here. With me. My baby . . .' His voice broke again and he looked away, pressing the heel of a hand into each of his eyes in turn. 'Aimee said she'd been snatched from a grocery store.' He shook his head. 'Didn't make any sense from the start. That woman never went to a grocery store in her life. Only a corner store for more cigarettes and beer. Besides, why'd she wait two days to call the police? She kept changing her story, too. First Bran was snatched from a cart. Then from the back of the car. She came to visit, all hopped up, told me crackpot stories, couldn't even bring herself to cry.' Harliss stared down at his hands, now clasped again. Gemma wondered how you could have faith after a loss like that. How you could pray.

'At first I thought Aimee might have just dumped her somewhere. Maybe even hurt her. The cops looked into it but not for long. They thought I was just mad, you know. The ex and all that. Aimee had a new guy, or at least it seemed like she did. She had a lot of money all of a sudden. New clothes, better car, and she was partying hard and heavy. Well.' For the first time, he smiled. But it was a horrible smile, thin and sharp and mean, like it had been cut there by a razor. 'She got hers, I guess. OD'd just a few months later. All that dirty money. It's true what the Bible says. You reap what you sow.'

'You think she sold Brandy-Nicole,' Gemma said, but Harliss took it as a question and nodded.

'I didn't know what to think, not then,' he said. 'But a few years later I saw the story of this woman, Monique White, who'd given over her kid to some group when she was a junkie and then cleaned up and tried to get the girl back. But the girl was gone. And she was only an hour from Durham, where we lived. Might not have thought much of it, except one of the hotshots on the board of the Home Foundation gave a quote, the woman was out of her mind, blah blah, the usual BS. *Saperstein*. The name jumped out at me. It was the same guy your dad had been writing to.'

Gemma was starting to see it. Dr. Saperstein, brilliant and ruthless and cruel. Her father, Mr. Moneybags, and his sudden change of heart. He must have been one of Haven's early investors, one of their *angel* investors.

Had he decided he wanted nothing to do with it as soon as Gemma came home? Or was it not until she started talking, started showing her defects, revealing imperfections that rendered her, in comparison to the daughter who'd died, so disappointing? And Richard Haven had been killed, maybe by Dr. Saperstein, maybe because Saperstein wanted to go from simply making clones to using them for bigger reasons. The institute was in danger of shutting down just when Saperstein got control of it. He must have been desperate.

'I don't understand.' That was Pete again, hugging himself, as if the room was cold, which it wasn't. It was stifling, airless. 'If Haven was making clones, why would they be after regular kids? What was the point?'

'Money,' Gemma said. Her voice squeaked. Harliss looked up at her, surprised, as if he'd forgotten she was there. Pete didn't look at her at all. 'Probably Saperstein wanted my dad's company to invest, to keep the institute on legs. Maybe they realized remaking dead kids for rich guys wasn't exactly a cash cow.' Pete cursed under his breath. Gemma got a raw pleasure in saying it. *Remaking dead kids.* The secret was out. She was a freak and a monster. There was no doubt about that now. 'Fine and Ives has always done a lot for the military. So Saperstein would have tried to prove the clones could be useful, to land a big contract. But if they couldn't afford to keep making them . . . Well, he took children he thought wouldn't be missed. He used them to test on. Just long enough to get the money he needed.'

'So there were normal kids at Haven,' Pete said, 'mixed in with the replicas.'

She couldn't even be angry that he'd called them normal. What else would they have been? 'Probably just in that first generation,' Gemma said. Harliss had said his daughter was roughly her age. 'Once Saperstein got the military contract through Fine and Ives, he wouldn't have taken the risk. Replicas are expensive, but they're disposable. At least, that's what everyone at Haven thought.' She thought of the way Lyra's hands trembled, her thinness, her confusion. She thought of the disease as if it were a kind of infestation, dark insects marching through Lyra's blood, nesting in the soft folds of her brain.

'All this time I thought maybe Bran was still out there,' Harliss said. He blinked back tears again. It made him look even more doglike, those big watery eyes and the wetness of his nose. 'Since I got sprung six weeks ago, I've been on the trail. After I saw *you*' – he nodded briefly in Gemma's direction, as though they'd met in North Carolina for tea – 'I thought I'd come down here myself to see it. I thought I could maybe find a way onto the island, see for myself what they were doing to those poor souls. But I was too late. I was too late. The flames were two, three stories high. Whoever burned it did it good.'

'I know,' Gemma said quietly. 'We saw it. We were there.'

Harliss shook his head. 'I didn't know what to do. This one woman, Emily Huang, kept cropping up in all the things I read about the Home Foundation. There was even a picture of her in one of the papers. And then I knew. I'd seen her one time with Aimee. It was at your house. She musta come around with Saperstein, but she spotted Aimee on the way out, started fussing over Brandy-Nicole. I thought I'd come to Palm Grove anyways, even though I heard all about how she strung herself up. What else could I do? And then there I was, sitting in my motel room and thinking about what to do next, and across the street I see *you*.' He looked up, amazed. 'It was like a sign. Like God saying I was on the right path.'

Gemma had almost forgotten that they weren't there by choice — that they'd been forced there, and that even now Harliss was within reach of the gun. She felt sorry for him, but that didn't mean she should trust him. He was desperate. That much was obvious. Desperate and with nothing to lose: a bad combination.

'Listen,' Gemma said. 'I saw the island. I got close to it. The whole institute's destroyed. There's nobody left. If your daughter really was at Haven, she's gone now. And I doubt you'll find her again.'

'Gemma.' Pete said her name quietly, but he might as well have been shouting.

But she didn't care. Everything was broken. And wasn't

it better to get it over with at once, to let the pain in, to let it take you? Wasn't it better than these years of puncture wounds and paper cuts, these chafing lies and half-truths, that left you rubbed raw and exposed? 'You have to give up,' Gemma said. 'I'm sorry. But you'll only be disappointed. It'll only break your heart.'

'It's too late for my heart anyway,' he said sharply, in a different tone. Fear and feeling came back to Gemma all at once when he stood up. But he moved away from her, turning his back. She thought about trying to take the gun but couldn't bring herself to reach for it. He stood there for a long time, facing the corner where the wall-paper was curling and a door gave entry to the cheap and shitty bathroom, and after a while when Gemma saw his shoulders moving she realized he was crying.

'When Bran was a baby, I was getting high with her mom and she somehow got out of her crib. Cracked her head open on a glass table. I'll never forget that. How much blood there was. Blood all over the carpet. She needed twenty stitches in her forehead. They almost took her away from us then.' He was losing it. 'I never got to say I'm sorry. I never got to tell her . . .' But he choked on whatever else he wanted to say.

Gem wanted to stand up and comfort him, but again she couldn't move. She was stilled by the memory of Lyra and the scar stitched above her right eyebrow. An ancient scar. Something she might have gotten as a baby.

'Mr. Harliss,' Gemma said. 'Do you have a picture of Brandy-Nicole?'

He turned around. His face was the color of a bruise. His upper lip shone with snot, and she was glad when he wiped it away with a sleeve. 'Yeah,' he said. He was getting control of himself again. 'Been carrying it with me since the day I went away the second time.' He brought an old leather wallet out of a pocket and began fishing around in the billfold. Gemma's arm in space looked like something foreign, something white and bloated and dead. Emma. The first one's name was Emma, and she was dead. 'Had more than this, but Aimee had 'em, so who knows where they went.'

The picture was small. The girl couldn't have been older than three. She was sitting on the floor in a blue dress and white tights, her brown hair clipped into pink barrettes, gripping a plastic cup decorated with parading lion silhouettes and grinning at someone to the left of the camera.

'That was only six months before she got took.' Mr. Harliss had moved to sit next to Gemma. Their thighs were practically touching. It was as though he'd forgotten how and why he'd brought them there. As if they were old friends, bound together by grief. 'She loved that cup,' he said. 'I remember Aimee yelled at her to put it down, but she wouldn't. She wouldn't go anywhere without that damn cup.'

The scar above the girl's eyebrow was more obvious than it was now. But it was unmistakably *her*.

Lyra, the replica, the lost child.

Gemma got to her feet. Parts of her body felt leaden, others impossibly light, as if she'd been disassembled and put back together wrong. All of a sudden, she thought her lungs were collapsing. She couldn't breathe. It was too hot. The air felt *wet* with heat, as if she was trying to inhale mud.

Peter squinted at her. 'Are you all right?' An idiotic question: she didn't think she'd ever be all right again.

'What?' Mr. Harliss said. 'What's wrong?'

She was going to throw up. She felt like she was relearning to walk, like she was just twitching across the room, like she might collapse. She half expected Mr. Harliss to stop her, but he didn't. 'What's wrong?' he was saying, 'What *is* it?' But she was at the door. She fumbled to release the chain and the dead bolt, her fingers clumsy-stiff, her body still rioting.

Then she was outside in air that was even worse, heavier, deader than the air inside. The sunshine felt like an insult. She leaned on the railing and stared down over the parking lot, heaving and coughing, trying to bring up whatever was lodged inside of her, that sick, twisted feeling in her guts, the horror of it. She wanted it out. But nothing came up. She was crying, too, all at once. The world went bright and the pain in her head narrowed to a fierce point and she was standing there in the stupid sun sobbing and snotting all over herself. A monster-girl. An alien. She was never meant to be here.

The door opened behind her. She didn't turn around. It would be Harliss, telling her to get back inside.

But it wasn't Harliss. Pete came to stand next to her. He put a hand on her elbow. 'Gemma?'

She pulled away from him. She knew she must look terrible. She always did when she cried, like something that had just been born, all red and slimy. Not that it mattered. He would never look at her the same way.

'Talk to me, Gemma,' he said.

The fact that he was still trying to be nice to her made her feel even worse.

'Don't,' she said. 'You don't have to.'

'Don't have to what?' Standing there in the afternoon sunlight, quiet and patient and sad, Pete looked like the most beautiful thing Gemma had ever seen. Like turning a corner, exhausted, lost, and seeing your house up ahead with all the lights on. Of course she would realize she was falling for him at the same time she would find out the truth about her parents and how she had been made from the sister who should have lived.

'You heard what he said.' Gemma couldn't bring herself to repeat the words. She squeezed the railing tightly, stupidly hoping she'd get a splinter, that she'd bleed some of this away. The parking lot was dazzling with sun and ugliness. 'You know what I am now.'

'What you *are*?' Pete reached out and placed a hand over hers. 'What are you talking about?'

She couldn't stand to have him touch her. She thought of her hand, her skin, grown in some laboratory. Was that how they did it? Did they culture her skin cells, like they would a yogurt, a bacteria? She took her hand away. 'I'm a freak,' she said. She couldn't stop crying. Jesus. 'I'm some kind of a monster.' Her heart was beating in her throat, making it hard to talk. 'The worst part is I think I always knew. I always *felt* it.'

'Gemma, *no*.' Pete grabbed her by her shoulders so she had no choice but to look at him. She wiped her face with a hand and left a slick trail of wet and maybe snot. Great. 'Listen to me, okay? Those men at Haven – the ones who stole children so they could get their funding, the ones who made people, living people, just to use them and poison them – those are the monsters, okay? Not you. You're amazing, do you hear me? You're perfect.'

Somehow through the suffocating mud of her misery, this penetrated. No one had ever told her she was perfect. She was about as far from perfect as you could get. And yet looking up at him, at his freckles and his eyes all warm with kindness, she believed that *he* thought so.

Of all the things that she'd seen and learned in the past week, this seemed like the most miraculous.

'So you don't hate me?' She swallowed a hiccup. She could only imagine what she looked like, but he didn't make her feel ugly. He still had his hands on her shoulders and she realized how close they were. No one had ever looked at her the way he was looking at her, or touched her like this, like she was something beautiful that needed preservation.

He smiled, and behind his eyes were doors that opened and said come in. 'God, Gemma. You really are dumb sometimes. You know that?'

He had to lean down a little to kiss her. Gemma had never felt small before in her life, but she did then: small and protected, held inside of the space made by his chest, by his hands on her cheeks. His lips were soft. He didn't try and put his tongue in her mouth and she was glad. It was her very first kiss and she was nervous, too nervous to have to sort out whether she was doing it right or worry about opening her mouth and whether she was using too much tongue or too little. She just wanted to stand there, in the sun, with the softness of his lips on hers and his fingers light on her cheeks. She moved her hands to his waist and felt the thrill of his body beneath the T-shirt, the narrowness of his waist, so delicious and foreign and other.

He pulled away and she took a step backward, bringing a hand to her lips, which were tingling. Her first kiss. With Pervy Pete. But she was happier than she could ever remember being. It felt like someone had cracked open a jar of honey in her chest. She was filled with a slow warmth.

'Wow,' he said. 'That was pretty good, huh?' His smile was so big she couldn't see beyond it.

She nodded, afraid to speak, afraid she would giggle.

'I mean, I'm not going to lie, I think I kind of killed it, actually. Like if there was a town for knowing when to kiss a girl, I'd probably be mayor.'

'Pete? Don't ruin it, okay?' But she was smiling, too. In the parking lot, a man in mirrored sunglasses was obviously watching them. She started to turn away, suddenly self-conscious – had he been staring at them the whole time, like some creep? – when she noticed the cut of his suit and the man, identically dressed and nearly invisible behind the glare of the windshield, sitting behind the driver's seat in the car next to him.

The car next to him was a maroon Volvo.

*The* maroon Volvo.

They'd been followed. They'd been found.

# FIFTEEN

ALL THE GOOD FEELING VANISHED. She was suddenly freezing.

'Two men,' she said.

As soon as he realized she'd spotted him, the man had
turned away, pretending to be talking on his cell phone.
'In the parking lot, watching us. They look military to
me. Don't look,' she said, grabbing Pete's wrist when he
started to turn.

'Military. Christ.' Pete had gone white again. Even his
freckles seemed to disappear. 'You sure?'

Gemma hated looking at the men. It felt like getting
slapped. But she did now, in time to see the guy in sunglasses once again pivot away from her the second her
eyes landed on him. He climbed into the car and for a
second she imagined – she prayed – they would simply
drive away. But both men just sat there. She nodded.

'How the hell did they find us?'

'I don't know.' She didn't know what they were waiting for. Maybe they didn't want to cause a scene. But she was positive the men, whoever they were, wouldn't let Pete and Gemma leave. Only an hour ago she'd been hoping for someone, anyone, to interfere with Harliss, to save them from him. But now she wished herself back inside that close-smelling room, back inside the dark with the gun.

'Look, what can they really do? I mean, think about it. We didn't do anything, right? They can't arrest us just for talking to Jake Witz. They're not going to throw us in jail. Sure, we broke a few traffic laws. Maybe they're here to give us a speeding ticket, no right turn signal, points off my license. . . .' He trailed off. She knew he didn't really believe that the men had followed them across Florida because they'd failed to signal.

Gemma saw movement in the parking lot. A hard slant of reflected sun. The car doors opened. Both men climbed out of the car. She heard a tinny ringing, and it took her a second to recognize her own ringtone. She fumbled her phone from her pocket. *Jake.*

'This is America,' Pete finished, in a whisper. As if that would help. As if that would protect them. 'I mean, they're not going to hurt us. They couldn't. They wouldn't. Right?'

Gemma felt a surge of relief, of joy. Jake would help them. He would know what to do. He was back on her side.

'Jake?' She nearly choked on the word. She was close to tears again. 'Is that you?'

It wasn't.

The girl's voice sounded distant, as if she was holding the phone away from her mouth.

'It's not Jake,' Lyra, who was really Brandy-Nicole, said. 'Jake is dead. And we need your help.'

*Jake is dead.*

Gemma's mind crystallized around this fact, even as she revolted against the truth of it. Jake Witz was dead. Jake: his dark eyes, the strange stillness of him, his sudden dazzling smiles that made you lose your breath.

Dead, dead, dead. Even the word was ugly.

Those men were responsible. If they hadn't done it themselves, they'd given the order. She knew it.

'Where are you?' she asked, and Lyra told her: the Blue Gator in Little Waller. Easy enough to remember.

'There's Suits after us,' Lyra said. 'Two of them.'

Her meaning was clear enough. They were being followed, too. 'Just stay where you are,' Gemma said. 'We're coming for you.' She hung up and slipped the phone back in her pocket.

Both of the men were pretending they weren't staring

up at room 33 – pretending there was something wrong with one of their tires, now, which required both of them to puzzle over it. Maybe they didn't know that Gemma had recognized them. Maybe that was why they weren't in a hurry. And of course they wouldn't want to make a scene, wouldn't want Gemma and Pete to start screaming and calling for help.

A scene. That's what they needed.

The phone call, both the news about Jake and the fact that Lyra and 72 weren't lost forever, had focused her. She knocked on the door of room 33, and Harliss opened up right away. He might have been standing at the door, listening, making sure they hadn't slipped away.

'Listen to me,' she said as soon as they were inside and the door was locked again behind them. 'I was wrong. Your daughter is still alive, and I know where to find her.'

Harliss took a step backward, as if she'd punched him. His hand worked its way to his chest. 'How – ?'

'There's no time to explain. We've been followed.' Gemma's mouth was chalk-dry. 'We need a distraction. The people who came for us won't like attention. They'll want us to come quietly. If we can get out of here, I can bring you to your daughter. I can protect her.'

'Fuck.' Pete turned a circle. But of course there was nowhere to go.

Harliss was staring at Gemma as if he'd never seen her before. She knew he hadn't heard a single thing she'd said. 'Brandy . . .' His voice was hushed with awe, like he was speaking inside a church. 'Where is she? Is she okay?'

Gemma fought down a hard swell of impatience. 'She's okay now,' she said. 'She won't be okay if those men out there get to her first.' He made a noise like a soccer ball punctured with a knife. 'Look, you were right. She's been living at Haven. They made up stories, told her she'd been made there.'

'All this time . . .' He shook his head. Although he must have expected it, he still looked as if someone had taken out his guts with a spoon. 'So she doesn't remember me? She doesn't remember anything about me at all?'

'She remembers a few things,' Gemma lied. How long would it be before the men got tired of waiting, and came up to finish the three of them off? She knew they'd killed Jake. She *felt* it. And she was sure they wouldn't have trouble killing again. 'Now *listen* to me. We need to get away from those men. We need your help. Your *daughter* needs your help.'

Harliss blinked. 'Okay.' He rubbed his face, as if trying to wake up from a dream. 'Where are they?'

'Down in the parking lot. Two of them. Maroon Volvo.'

His eyes were still raw-red, as though they'd been

scoured. 'You're not messing with me? You know where my girl is?'

'I swear,' Gemma said.

'And if I help you, you'll help me?'

Gemma nodded. Harliss turned to look at Pete. Pete held up both hands.

'Yes, yes,' he said quickly. 'Just . . . Christ. Let's get out of here, okay?'

Harliss ignored that. He turned back to Gemma. 'Now *you* listen to me.' He took a step forward and Gemma flinched, expecting him to grab her. But he only brought his finger up to point. 'You get my girl. You bring her back to me safe, okay? You take her home to North Carolina until I get out.'

'Get out?' she said. Her chest was tight with fear. 'Get out of what? Aren't you coming with us?'

But Harliss didn't answer. He gave Gemma one final look and then moved past her to retrieve the gun from the bedside table. Before she could ask him what he intended to do, he'd slipped out the door. She could tell he was moving away from room 33 by the sound of his voice, which came back to them through the thin walls. He was shouting, letting off a volley of slurred obscenities and even snatches of song.

Pete went to the window and parted the curtains to look out. 'He's pretending to be drunk or something,' he said. 'He's stumbling all over the place.'

'Smart,' Gemma said. That would get at least the desk clerk to pay attention. Maybe the other guests, if there *were* any.

'Should we call the police?' Pete asked.

'And say what? Some military guys are trying to kill us because they've been cloning people to use as petri dishes?' Gemma shook her head. They needed to get to Little Waller, fast. They didn't have time to tangle with cops and questions like *Where are your parents?*

'I don't know.' Pete was pacing the room. 'Even if those guys are military, they can't do anything with cops around, right?'

He was right. They needed cops, firemen, a whole shit-show drama. But they couldn't call. Something hinged open in her chest – an idea, a *hope*. She grabbed Pete's hand and dragged him into the bathroom.

'Seems like the wrong time for a shower,' he said. But his voice was unsteady, breaking on the joke. 'Aren't we supposed to be getting out of here?'

There was no escape this way. Nothing but a single slit of a window barely the width of a pizza box. She registered the sad shower, the sink with a nest of hair clinging like a waterlogged insect to the basin, the fire alarm. She grabbed the roll of toilet paper from next to the toilet and threw it in the sink.

Pete stood there, staring. 'What are you . . . ?'

'Quick,' she said. 'I need a lighter or matches or something.' She bent to search the cabinet beneath the sink. Several sheets of old newspaper lined the plywood. She balled them up and threw that in the basin, too.

Then he got it. He disappeared again into the bedroom, returning with a sheet from one of the beds and a book of matches from a place called Skins. There were only three matches left.

'Dresser drawer,' he said, tossing them to Gemma. 'Someone always leaves them behind.'

She was so nervous she took off the first match head when she tried to strike it. But she got the second one lit. The newspaper flared and curled. The toilet paper began to smoke.

'Shut the door,' she said, as the smoke began to drift out toward the bedroom, sniffing for oxygen. Pete stepped inside, closing the door behind him, and together they blew softly on the fire, so flames leapt up toward the mirror from the sink. Gemma's eyes watered. The chemicals in the paper let off an acrid smell.

The fire alarm was much louder than Gemma had expected. She plugged her fingers in her ears. The bathroom was now so full of smoke, her eyes began to water. Finally they couldn't stand it anymore and opened the door to the bedroom, stumbling out, coughing and sucking in clean air. There must have been a sprinkler system fitted at one point, but it hadn't been maintained. A dribble of water came from a thin pipe in the ceiling, and did nothing but wet the carpet. Already Gemma heard the wail of sirens in the distance. She hadn't thought there'd be so much smoke. . . .

'Shit.' Pete had his shirt to his mouth. He had to cough out the word. 'The walls.'

The wallpaper in the bathroom had caught fire. Gemma had never seen anything like it. She'd never been so close to a fire at home, sitting in front of the fireplace, and those were the gas kind that ran on a neat little grate tucked away behind fake logs. Click on, click off. But now through the open door of the bathroom she saw the fire climbing the walls, leaping onto the plastic shower curtain and simply devouring it. She had the strangest urge to run back and try to smother it – as if she could do anything – and then fear hooked her hard in the stomach. *Out.* They needed to get out. The sirens outside were louder now. A bit of the carpet caught fire and the flame made a hand, waggled its fingers at her, crawled a little farther into the bedroom.

They couldn't get the door open. For a horrible second, she thought the men had somehow trapped them, locked Gemma and Pete inside so that their job would be easy. Then she realized that in his panic Pete had locked the bolt instead of unlocking it, and she reached up and slammed the bolt free and wrenched the door open. The fire made a sound – like a roar, like an animal, like it was alive and hungry – and smoke came out with them, clouds of it. But they were now in the sunshine, on the balcony, and she saw a cop car below them in the parking lot, newly arrived, and a fire truck just pulling in, and a dozen people slowly drifting into the street to watch. A crowd.

She saw things in images, pictures and flashes. In the parking lot: a teenage girl holding a kid – her son? – by the hand, her son trying to fit an enormous lollipop in his mouth. The desk clerk talking on his phone, an old woman pointing, athletic socks bunched around her ankles. A boy was standing next to the maroon Volvo, angling his phone toward the balcony, filming. Time was moving very quickly for Gemma, so everything else seemed almost to be frozen. The agony of the fire truck angling into the parking lot. The sludge of a cop getting out of his car.

'Don't you try and tell me what to do. I know your type. You keep your hands *off* me.'

The mouth of the stairwell: fifty feet away, Harliss, stumbling and still pretending to be drunk, so the two men in suits were forced to dance around him. Gemma sliced the scene into segments, into *instinct*. They did not want to use violence, had been trying to get him to go quietly. He was shouting, shaking off one of the men, who had a hand on his elbow.

'I know my rights. This is America. I know all about the Constitution. . . .'

There was no way down to the parking lot but past them. And as Gemma and Pete stood there, maybe for half a second, maybe less, one of the men turned and saw them. He still hadn't taken off his sunglasses, and that was the scariest thing, worse even than a fire that obeyed its natural impulse to burn – the unnaturalness of a man doing what he had come to do and yet not bothering to take off his sunglasses, *no reason to sweat, no reason to get upset.*

And in that second she knew, she truly understood, what Pete had said to her outside. Monsters weren't made, at least not by birth or fate or circumstance. Monsters chose to be monsters. That was the only terrible birth, the kind that happened again and again, every day.

He was coming toward them. And still the endless sludge of firefighters half suited up, the radio static, the cop dull and useless standing there. The man couldn't take them, not if she screamed, not if she fought. There would be too much attention, too many questions, a cop coming to pull them aside and ask awkward questions. But they might lose Lyra and 72. Every minute, she was in danger of losing them.

He was close enough to speak, above the roar and Har-liss's shouting and the way that things hum into sound as they're collapsing. 'It will be easier, and much better, if you come with me,' he was saying. 'You're in a lot of dan-ger. I'm here to help.' Not the words Gemma had been expecting, but she still picked up on the lie, the worst kind – the kind that pretends to be a favor. She'd been hearing them her whole life.

'We're not going anywhere,' Pete said, stepping in front of Gemma as if he could protect her, a gesture so sweetly useless she wanted to cry.

They were mirrored in his sunglasses, the two of them. She thought of shattering those glasses and the eyes beneath them, too. His face dissolving. Her fists like superhero hands, extending into trunks, pummeling him.

'You don't understand,' he said. 'I'm on your side.' He took a step forward. He reached for Pete. 'I'm going to have to insist –'

The gunshot was a clean, sharp crack that cleaved the air in two. Gemma had heard people describe gunshots as cars backfiring, as firecrackers, but she had no doubt what this was, even before she saw Harliss, still in that strange snapshot way, holding the gun, the barrel pointed to the sky. There seemed to be a pause before people were screaming, although she knew there was no pause, really: there was a gun and a shot and the man holding

Harliss had dropped to the ground, and the man standing in front of Pete, telling them he was only trying to help, had dropped, too, because of course they couldn't do anything else.

Harliss fired a second shot. Now dozens of people were screaming. Half the people in the parking lot were lying down, or ducking behind cars. For a split second Gemma met Harliss's eyes and the message felt physical, like the first inhale after the breath is knocked from your lungs. She understood why he'd asked her to keep Lyra safe until he was out. She understood that he'd waited more than a decade to see his daughter again and would now go back to prison because of the promise a stranger had made to him, because of the sheerest, slightest chance that it might help.

There was no time, only change, only atoms rotating, only Gemma and Pete and Rick Harliss and a love so turned around and imperfect and blind it could only be called faith. Things that existed outside of seconds and minutes and years. Gemma was peaceful now. She was calm. Both men were still on the ground and the cop was running for the staircase with two firefighters behind him – and yet Gemma saw them, suspended, still, held in that moment by a force much larger and more patterned than they were – and the little kid had dropped his lollipop to scream. There were more sirens in the distance.

Then they were down the stairs and through the crowd in the parking lot and almost at the van. They were beyond the swell of bodies, of voices, of people shouting and crying. They were in a universe made infinitely of itself, and yet small enough to hold these moments, these facts – the smell of smoke in the air, the echo of voices, and Pete's hand, bigger than hers, stronger, right.

# SIXTEEN

GEMMA WISHED THEY COULD DITCH the van and
trade it for something less conspicuous. She felt like they
were driving around in a giant neon sign. But they made
it back to Little Waller without seeing the maroon Volvo.
As far as Gemma could tell, they hadn't been followed.

It had been more than an hour and Gemma was terrified that Lyra and 72 might have left, or been taken.
They found the replicas huddled in a booth in the back of
a restaurant called the Blue Gator, with paper shamrocks
strung between the televisions and green vinyl booths and
*Kiss Me, I'm Irish* T-shirts for sale behind the bar. They
were in trouble: 72 was scowling at the table, and a waiter
was badgering them to put in an order.

'I told you, it's not up to me.' The waiter had bad dan-
druff that coated the shoulders of his black T-shirt. 'It's
restaurant policy. These booths are for diners, and that

means people *dining* –'

'It's all right.' Gemma noticed that Lyra's face transformed when she pushed through the crowd – Lyra actually looked happy. It was amazing how in such a short time, Gemma felt responsible for this skinny little rag doll with her big eyes and terrible past. Brandy-Nicole. 'They're with us, and we're leaving.'

'You weren't followed?' Gemma asked them, as soon as they were safely back in the car. Pete got on the highway immediately, although they hadn't agreed on a destination. Easier to disappear on the big roads, in the big towns.

Lyra shook her head. 'We were,' she said. 'But not there. Not into that place.'

'A man looked in from the street,' 72 said. 'But he didn't see us.'

Above them, the sky was shedding its blue, revealing an undercoat of improbable violets and pinks. Gemma found herself praying that the night, and the darkness that transformed cars to headlights and absorbed individual features, would come quickly. She didn't want to ask about Jake – on one level, she didn't want to know – but it was far too late to pretend, and she owed it to Jake to face up to the truth of what had been done to him. 'What happened to Jake?'

Lyra was the one who told them the whole story: about

tracking down Emily Huang and learning she was dead, about finding Jake's address and deciding to go and speak to him, about the man and woman who'd come to clean up the job.

'Both of them strung up, made to look like suicides.' Gemma's mouth tasted bitter, as if she'd inhaled ash along with the smoke earlier, and she couldn't stop coughing. 'Must be the military's little specialty.'

'Less suspicious, maybe, than a gun,' Pete said quietly. He reached out and put a hand on her knee. Her heartbeat responded, jumped a little beneath his touch. That, at least, was one good thing, maybe the only good thing to come out of this: Pete was hers.

'Why did you run?' Gemma asked, and for a second neither Lyra nor 72 spoke.

'It was Caelum's idea . . . ,' Lyra said finally.

'Caelum?' Gemma twisted around in her seat and was shocked to see that 72 was actually smiling, staring out the window, as if the smear of highways contained the world's best secret. She hadn't seen him smile before – wouldn't have even said he was capable of smiling – and she was shocked by the change. He'd gone instantly from *brooding sociopath* to *budding Calvin Klein model*.

'I named him,' Lyra said proudly. 'Like Dr. O'Donnell named me.'

'I wasn't sure I could trust you.' The boy now named

Caelum turned away from the window to meet Lyra's eyes. 'I'm sorry.' She wondered whether the act of naming him had changed him on deeper levels, too. She couldn't imagine this boy, the boy sitting politely in the backseat wearing a Seven-Up T-shirt, pulling a knife on them in a swamp.

'And I almost forgot.' Lyra unzipped a backpack Gemma knew she must have stolen from April's grandparents' guesthouse. 'Before she died, Nurse Em gave three pieces of art to her next-door neighbor. I found these hidden in the backing.' She passed Lyra two printouts and one handwritten sheet of names. Gemma's stomach turned over. *Brandy-Nicole Harliss* was the third name on the list, but there were forty-seven others. That might mean that all these names, all these children, had been taken from their parents or from foster homes when Haven was in danger of running out of funding, used as bodies before new bodies could be manufactured.

'Can I keep these?' Gemma asked, and Lyra shrugged, although she saw the expression of hunger there – it was the same way Lyra had stared at the bookshelves, like a starving person confronted with a feast. 'I'll give them back, I promise.' There was no point in delaying anymore: she had to tell Lyra about her father. She didn't know why she felt so nervous. Lyra would probably be happy. She would be happy. She had a dad, which meant she probably had other family out there – cousins, aunts. 'There's something I need to tell you, Lyra. Something about your past.'

'*Now?*' Pete said. 'Here?'

Gemma pivoted to look at him. 'What's the point in waiting?'

'What?' Lyra said. When Gemma turned around again, she noticed that Caelum and Lyra were holding hands. Or not holding hands, exactly – they were touching palm to palm as if they *wanted* to hold hands but didn't quite know how to do it. 'What is it?'

Gemma took a deep breath. The sun was bleeding red on the horizon. 'You weren't actually made at Haven.'

'What do you mean?' It was Caelum who spoke. There was an edge to his voice. Not anger, Gemma thought. Fear. 'Where was she made?'

'Nowhere.' Gemma hadn't realized how hard it would be to explain. 'This list, and all the names on it? I'm pretty sure these are all kids who got taken from their families or from foster care and were brought to Haven, at a time the institute couldn't afford to keep making human models.' Lyra was sitting there huge-eyed, white-faced, and Gemma had the sudden urge to apologize, to take it all back. But that was insane. Maybe she simply didn't understand? 'The third name, Brandy-Nicole Harliss. That was your birth name. Your *real* name. That was the name your parents gave you.'

'My . . .' Lyra inhaled whatever else she was going to say.

'You have parents,' Gemma said. She thought Lyra might cry, or laugh, or at the very least, smile. But she just kept staring, looking horrified, as if Gemma had opened up a coffin to show her a dead body. 'Well, you have a father. He's been looking for you all this time. He's loved you all this time.'

Lyra cried out, as if she'd been hit. And Caelum, Gemma noticed, withdrew his hand from Lyra's, and turned back to the window.

# SEVENTEEN

IT WAS TIME TO GO home. They had no options left. Gemma would have to confront her parents. Strangely, the idea no longer frightened her. She felt she'd aged years in the past few days. She felt only a vague pity when she thought of her father, and the secret he'd been carrying all these years, and the dead child they had refused to mourn. For her father and mother thinking they could buy their way out of tragedy.

She would go home, but on her terms: no more lies.

By eleven o'clock Pete could hardly stay awake at the wheel. They weren't far from Savannah when they passed an RV park and campground, Gemma suggested they stop for the night. She didn't mind spending one more night on the road. She knew that everything would change in the morning. She had an idea that her life would never be the same, that she'd never go back to worrying about

Chloe and Aubrey and the pack wolves, that she'd never spend another gym class sitting miserably in the bleachers, fudging her way through math homework.

She had a feeling this was her last free night.

The campground was enormous and surprisingly full. Gemma estimated there were at least four dozen tour bus–size RVs and even more smaller camper vans, plus tents peaked like angular mushrooms across the sparse grass. It was a beautiful night, and outside there was a feeling of celebration. Old couples sat side by side on lawn chairs dragged out onto the cracked asphalt, drinking wine from paper cups. Children ran between the tents, and a group of twentysomethings with long dreads and bare feet were cooking on a portable camper stove. Fireflies flared sporadically in the darkness, and people shouted to one another and shared beers and stories of where they were going and where they'd come from.

Pete left in search of food from the gas station, and Caelum moved off in the direction of the pay-per-use stalls, walking slightly ahead of Lyra. Gemma suspected he wanted to be left alone, but she followed them at a safe distance, half-believing that they might once again simply melt into the darkness. But after Lyra took money for the showers she knew she could no longer delay the inevitable. It was time to call home.

She'd missed thirty-seven calls from her parents. When

she pulled up her texts, she saw they progressed from furious to frenzied to desperate.

*Please,* her father had written. *Wherever you are, please call us.* He must have come back early from his business trip. That meant things had really gone nuclear.

She dialed her dad's cell phone number and he picked up on the first ring.

'Gem?' He sounded frantic, so unlike himself that her resolution faltered. 'Gem, is that you? Are you there?'

'I'm here, Dad.' She had to hold her phone away from her ear when Kristina started shouting in the background. *Is that her? Where is she? Is she okay? Let me talk to her. . . .* 'Look, I'm fine. I'm not hurt.'

'Where are you? Jesus Christ, we've been so worried –'

'Geoff, let me talk to her.' Kristina's voice, slurry from crying and maybe from pills, was audible again in the background.

'Hang on, Gem, I'm putting you on speakerphone. Your mother wants to hear your voice.' Fumbling, and the echo of her parents' voices overlapping. Gemma hated speakerphone, which always made her feel as if she was speaking into a tin can. 'Gemma, are you still there? Can you hear us?'

'I can hear you,' she said. 'There's no need to shout.' She watched a mom bouncing a sleepy toddler in her arms, passing back and forth in front of the RV, the kid's dark hair curling on her shoulder. She felt a momentary grief so strong it was like falling.

'Where are you?' Kristina sounded like she was crying again. 'We've been so worried. We called April and she said you'd left. Your father jumped on the first plane out of London he could find. She was so upset –'

'April was upset?' Gemma asked quickly.

'What do you think? She told us you had a fight and she'd asked you to leave. She felt awful about it. She's been worried sick. We've all been worried sick.'

'I'm fine,' Gemma said. 'I'm with my friend Pete. We'll be home tomorrow.'

'I want you home *tonight*,' Gemma's father said, sounding more like himself. Now that he knew his daughter wasn't dead in a ditch, he'd apparently decided to resort to playing bad cop. 'Where are you? I'm coming to get you.'

It was time. She took a breath. 'I went down to see Haven.'

There was a long moment of silence. Gemma watched the fireflies flare and then go dark.

'You . . . what?' Gemma's dad could barely get the words out.

'I went to Haven.' She closed her eyes and thought of the statue of the man kneeling in the dust, that old childhood memory unearthed, the DNA of another child coiled inside of her. 'I went to see where I was made.'

'Where you . . .' Geoff's voice cracked, and he cleared his throat. 'What — what are you talking about?'

'There's no point in denying it. I know everything.' She was suddenly and completely exhausted. She felt so old — older, even, than her parents. 'I know about what you were trying to do at Haven. I know you left Fine and Ives because they wanted to invest. I know the military stepped in and the mission changed.' Gemma's mom whimpered. This part would be the hardest. 'I know about Emma, too,' she said.

Her parents were quiet for so long she checked the phone to see whether the connection had been lost. Finally she heard a kind of gasping and knew that they were still there. She imagined the lies they'd told over the years as a physical force, something with hands, something that had reached out now to choke them.

'Gemma.' Her father was crying. Her father had *never* cried, not once in her life. She was shocked and also, in a sick way, glad. The mask was falling off. The cracks were showing. Let him cry, the way she had. 'We can explain. Please. You need to come home.'

'Please come home, baby.' Kristina sounded like her voice was being squeezed through a pipe, high and agonized, and Gemma felt terrible again. Even now, she hated for her mother to be sad. But Gemma knew she had to be strong.

'Not until you agree to help me,' she said. In the distance she saw Pete returning from the direction of the gas station with a paper bag tucked under his arm. As he passed beneath the streetlamp and back into the RV park, a man smoking a cigarette nearby turned to look at him, and Gemma had a tingling sense of unease. But the man turned away again and was soon lost to Gemma's view. 'You have to help my friends, too.'

'Your friends?'

'We rescued two replicas out on the marshes,' Gemma said. Once again she had to yank her phone away from her ear as both of her parents exploded. She nearly had to shout to be heard over them. 'They would have died on their own. They *are* dying. Haven's been infecting them.'

'Listen to me, Gemma. You're in danger right now.' Gemma's father was calm again, and she felt a swell of nausea. He hadn't even reacted to the news about how Haven was using its clones. Which meant, of course, that he knew. She wasn't surprised, but it still made her feel sick. Had he known, too, about the children stolen from their parents, shunted into the foster care system and then conveniently lost? 'I know you must be angry. I can only imagine how you feel. I swear to you that your mother and I will explain. But you need to come home now. Tonight. There are people out there, people still involved in Haven, dangerous people. . . . I can't protect you when you're hundreds of miles away.'

She thought of Nurse Em, and Jake, both found swinging by their necks. 'You have to swear to help us, or I'm not coming home at all,' she said. It was a bluff. She had nowhere to go, and if her parents cut off her credit cards she'd be doubly screwed, but she was counting on the fact that her parents were too upset to think clearly.

'This isn't a game, Gemma.' Geoff sounded as if he was going to lose it. Gemma had never heard her father so out of control. 'You don't understand how big this is —'

'Swear or I hang up the phone,' she said firmly.

For a second there was nothing but the sound of her father breathing hard on the other end of her line, of her mom whimpering in the background.

'I swear,' he said at last. 'I'll do everything I can.'

Gemma exhaled. She'd unconsciously been holding her breath. 'I'll be home in the morning,' she said, and hung up. Immediately she powered off her phone. She didn't want them calling her back, bugging her all night. She leaned against Pete's minivan, listening to the sounds of the mothers calling their children to bed, watching lights dim one by one in the windows of parked RVs. All these people on their way to something, on their way from something. All these stories and lives, all of them orbiting temporarily around the same parking lot before spinning away from one another again. She said a little prayer for Jake Witz.

She thought of her sister – could Emma be called a sister, if she was really Gemma, if Gemma was really her? – and the shadow-life she might have lived, might still be living off in some parallel dimension.

She felt small. She was so tired.

Pete was back. He'd bought water and soda, candy and chips, burritos, and even a tray of gas station nachos. 'I thought we'd do a buffet,' he said, squatting to place food out right on the pavement. When he saw Gemma's face, he stopped. 'What's the matter?'

'Nothing,' she said. 'Just tired. Just scared about what comes next.'

He stood up. Backlit by the lights from a nearby camper, his face was unreadable, and his hair looked feather-light. He reached out and touched her cheek, and his hand was so warm, so instantly familiar. A strange and baffling truth: that the people we're supposed to know best can turn out to be strangers, and that near strangers can feel so much like home.

'We'll be okay,' he said, and she loved that, loved hearing him say *we*, loved being a part of him. He traced a thumb lightly over her cheekbones, and where he touched her she felt beautiful. Like he was sewing up the ugly parts. He smiled, that goofy smile Gemma couldn't believe she hadn't always been in love with. 'Just think about it. Clones at school. *Real* clones, not just Chloe and the rest of her drones.'

'Yeah.' Gemma forced a smile. It was a fantasy. Lyra and Caelum would never go to school. If they wanted to stay alive, they'd likely have to go underground, stay hidden, stay on the run. And they would only get sicker. But it was a nice idea and she didn't want to spoil it.

'Go to sleep,' Pete said more quietly. He leaned forward and touched his lips to hers, but just that light pressure made her whole body shiver. 'I'll keep watch for a bit.'

With the backseats folded down, the minivan was more than big enough to lie down in. Pete had a blanket, too, and he insisted she use his sweatshirt as a pillow.

'Good night, Gemma.' Pete leaned over to kiss her again. This time, he let his lips stay longer, and she felt his warmth on top of her, the impossible and delicious solidity of his body. The bones and blood and skin that separate but also bring us back together. The gift of them.

Even though she was tired, she didn't think she'd be able to sleep, not after everything that had happened. But she did.

Sometime later she woke up because Pete was shaking her.

'Someone's coming,' he said.

She sat up. The darkness was gummy-thick, and her whole body felt sticky. The rear door was still open, letting in the noise of tree frogs and the occasional muffled sound of a door opening and closing as people went or returned from the bathroom. She didn't know what time it was, but she couldn't have been asleep very long. Pete didn't look as if he'd slept at all. He was wide awake, alert, staring.

He pointed at the beam of a flashlight moving between the parked vans. She could tell from the pattern it made that whoever was out there was making a tour of each vehicle, as if looking for something specific.

Looking for *someone* specific.

'Where's Lyra?' Gemma whispered. Her body was electric with fear. 'Where's Caelum?'

'Outside,' Pete said. 'Sleeping.'

How on earth could they have been followed? Gemma was sure they had been careful, switching highways, watching constantly for cars that seemed to be pursuing them. Maybe, she thought, someone was monitoring her phone calls. She'd seen stuff like that on the cop shows on TV, how police could triangulate phone calls to find wanted criminals. Hunted. That was what she felt like — like an animal crouching in a hole, just waiting to be torn apart.

There was no way she could wake Lyra and Caelum

and get them in the car without being seen. Already the flashlight – and the person behind it – was less than twenty feet away, moving around an RV that belonged to an older couple Gemma had spoken to earlier. There was no tearing out of here, either, not in the dark, not without risking mowing down some poor dad on his way to the toilet or kids sleeping in a tent.

'Lie down,' Gemma said. Their best bet was to pretend to be asleep and pray they would be passed over – that in the darkness they wouldn't be recognized. Pete had covered her with a blanket and she drew this up over their faces, so the sound of their breathing was amplified beneath it. She was too scared to process even how close they were lying, his knees pressed to her knees, his chest rising and falling with his breath and their noses practically touching.

But no sooner had they lain down than she heard a voice.

'Gemma? Gemma?'

Instantly, she sat up again, half-delirious, disbelieving. She *knew* that voice.

'*April?*' she whispered.

'Oh my God, *Gemma*. Thank God.' The flashlight thudded to the ground and for a quick second, as April bent to retrieve it, revealed her familiar green Converses. 'Shit. Where *are* you?'

Gemma shook off the blanket and scooted out of the van. She felt clumsy with happiness. 'I'm here,' she said, and the flashlight swept over her and held her momentarily in its light. 'I'm right here.' She held out both arms and a second later, April was rocketing into them.

'I was so worried about you,' she said, nearly taking Gemma off her feet. 'I was so mad, you know – Latin temper and all that – but then a few hours after I left the house I started feeling really, really awful. Like my-stomach-is-trying-to-eat-itself awful. And I came home, and you were gone already, and then your parents called me. . . .'

'How did you find me?' Gemma was half tempted to touch April's hair and nose and shoulders, to doubly make sure she was real.

'Find My Phone app, duh,' April said. Gemma almost laughed. Of course. 'But then you turned your phone off, and then of course as soon as I got here *my* phone ran out of charge. So I've been walking around like a total perv, peeking in people's windows. . . . *Perv?*' she squeaked, as Pete climbed out of the van.

Gemma was glad that it was so dark she couldn't make out April's expression. 'April, you know *Pete*,' she said, deliberately emphasizing the name and hoping that April would take the hint. 'Pete was the one who drove me down to Florida.'

'Uh-huh.' April seemed momentarily speechless, a

first for her. Gemma could practically see her making calculations – the size of the van, the fact that both Gemma and Pete had been sleeping inside, *together*. 'Where are the . . . others?' She was deliberately avoiding the word *clones*, and Gemma remembered what they'd fought about, and what she'd now have to confess to April: that she was one of them. Made. Manufactured. She would have to tell April about her parents' first child, the lost child she'd been made to replicate. She would have to tell April about Rick Harliss and Jake Witz's murder. She was hit by a wave of exhaustion again. This was the world she lived in now.

As if he knew what she was thinking, Pete put his arm around her. 'They're sleeping,' he said. 'They're okay.'

Gemma leaned into him, grateful, not even caring what April thought. 'We're all okay,' she said. She reached for April's hand and gave it a squeeze. There in the darkness, in the middle of nowhere, her boyfriend and her best friend: under the circumstances, she could hardly ask for more.

# EIGHTEEN

APRIL SLEPT IN HER CAR. For most of the night, Pete kept his arm around Gemma's waist, breathing into her hair, and she woke surprisingly refreshed, considering the fact that she was lying with her cheek squashed against the van's scratchy carpeting and one whole arm was numb.

It was just after six o'clock. She eased out of the van and saw that Lyra and Caelum were still sleeping, their bodies tented under a blanket pulled all the way over their heads. Beneath it they appeared to be one person. She showered and brushed her teeth in the semi-slimy bathroom, next to little kids giddy with the experience of camping and their bleary-eyed moms. Afterward, she woke April, and they went in search of breakfast from the little mini-mart and gas station where Pete had bought all the junk food the night before. They bought hot coffee and muffins the texture of sponges, but were so hungry they didn't care.

They ate at a picnic bench slick with dew and watched the sun beat the mist off the ground. It was going to be another beautiful day.

Gemma told April everything. When she explained what had happened to Jake Witz, she realized she was trying not to cry. But she forced herself to keep talking. She told April about what she'd learned from Rick Harliss, about what her parents had done after their first child had died. About why and how she'd been made. By then she *was* crying, not even because she felt sorry for herself, but weirdly because she mourned the child, Emma. She even felt sorry for her parents. They must have grieved. They must have been grieving for years. What would it be like to look at your daughter and see a perfect reflection of a child you'd lost?

To her credit, April didn't freak out. She waited until Gemma was finished, and then she scooted closer on the bench to give Gemma a hug. April gave the best hugs. Even though Gemma was much larger than April was, somehow April made her feel totally enfolded, totally taken care of.

'I'm proud of you, bug,' April said, using an old nickname, which made Gemma laugh and cry harder at the same time.

Gemma pulled away. 'Jeez. I'm like a snot factory,' she said.

'I hear there's big money in snot nowadays.'

Gemma laughed again, choking a bit, wiping her face with a sleeve. 'Do you think I'll ever feel normal again?'

April snorted. 'Come on, Gemma. When did we ever feel normal?' She nudged Gemma's shoulder. 'We're aliens, remember?'

'You're an alien,' Gemma said. 'I'm a clone.'

'*The Adventures of Alien and Clone*. Sounds like a Marvel movie. I'm in,' April said. And then, in a different voice, 'Besides, normal is overrated. Normal is a word invented by boring people to make them feel better about being boring.'

'Maybe you're right.' Gemma did, in fact, feel a little better. A little lighter. She was still dreading going home to confront her parents, but she knew she couldn't delay it forever. The sun had risen. The sky was the color of a Creamsicle, and full of whipped-cream clouds. She stood up. 'We should probably wake the others.'

'No way. Uh-uh. You skipped over the most important part of the story.' April grabbed Gemma's wrist and hauled her down onto the bench again. She was grinning, shark-wide, the way she did. 'So,' she said, leaning forward on an elbow. "Fess up. What's the deal with you and Perv?'

They were on the road by ten. April followed the van in her car, occasionally tooting her horn or pulling up alongside the van to wave or give a thumbs-up. Pete kept up a constant stream of conversation, as usual, but this time he spoke mostly to Lyra and Caelum, trying to explain all about the world they hardly knew.

'Strip malls are like the arteries of America. They keep the whole country alive. Pizzerias, nail salons, shitty hardware stores . . . this is it, you know? The pinnacle of human achievement. If we ever get to Mars, I bet we'll build a nail salon first thing.'

Mostly, Gemma listened. Mostly, she turned her face to the window and saw her double reflected there, ghostly over the passing landscape: a different Gemma from the one who'd left home less than a week ago – stronger, both more and less sure of herself. She didn't know what was coming for her, but she knew that she'd be ready. They were safe for now. They were together. She had April and Pete. Lyra had her. Caelum had a name.

And despite what she'd said to April, she felt a little less alien than she had before. A little smarter. A little more amazed, too, by all the mysteries she'd seen, by the complexity of the universe and the people inside of it.

A little more human, even.

A NEW THRILLER, AVAILABLE FROM JULY 2012

# Guilty Wives

## James Patterson
## & David Ellis

**Four best friends on a decadent vacation – thrown in prison for murder.**

**No husbands allowed**

Only minutes after Abbie Elliot and her three best friends step off of a private helicopter, they enter the most luxurious, sumptuous, sensually pampering hotel they have ever been to. Their lavish presidential suite overlooks Monte Carlo, and they surrender: to the sun and pool, to the sashimi and sake, to the Bruno Paillard champagne. For four days they're free to live someone else's life. As the weekend moves into pulsating discos, high-stakes casinos, and beyond, Abbie is transported to the greatest pleasure and release she has ever known.

**What happened last night?**

In the morning's harsh light, Abbie awakens on a yacht, surrounded by police. Something awful has happened – something impossible, unthinkable. Abbie, Winnie, Serena, and Bryah are arrested and accused of the foulest crime imaginable. And now the vacation of a lifetime becomes the fight of a lifetime – for survival.

*Guilty Wives* is the ultimate indulgence, the kind of non-stop joy-ride of excess, friendship, betrayal, and danger that only James Patterson can create.

$$\overline{C}$$

Century · London

# JAMES PATTERSON

To find out more about James Patterson
and his bestselling books, go to
www.jamespatterson.co.uk